SEARCHING
FOR CELIA

Visit us at www.boldstrokesbooks.com

By the Author

The Remarkable Journey of Miss Tranby Quirke

Searching for Celia

SEARCHING FOR CELIA

by
Elizabeth Ridley

2015

SEARCHING FOR CELIA

ISBN 13: 978-1-62639-356-1

This Trade Paperback Original Is Published By
Bold Strokes Books, Inc.
P.O. Box 249
Valley Falls, NY 12185

First Edition: June 2015

CREDITS
EDITOR: RUTH STERNGLANTZ
PRODUCTION DESIGN: SUSAN RAMUNDO
COVER DESIGN BY GABRIELLE PENDERGRAST

Acknowledgments

Thanks to everyone who helped make this book possible, especially Adam Pernak for a "spin around the wheel," Trish Hindley, everyone at Bold Strokes Books for being so great at what they do, and special thanks to Claudius and Calpurnia, just for being such consistently fantastic cats.

Dedication

For Yaya, so she'll stop bugging me to write a mystery...

The heart of the person before you is a mirror.
See there your own form.

—Shinto

CHAPTER ONE

Wednesday, March 23
6:42 a.m.

The talkative Belgian at my elbow concerns me more than the potential terrorist across the aisle in seat 46D. Sure, 46D could kill all of us onboard this loaded 747 at any moment, but the Belgian's incessant speculation about our deaths has me truly frightened. "Ze air would rush from ze cabin, of course, in ze first few moments…"

Ignoring the Belgian, I pray. *And there went a man of the house of Levi, and took to wife a daughter of Levi…*

46D is ringed with sweat. His heavy-lidded eyes dart to the overhead luggage rack; muscles spasm in his neck.

And the woman conceived, and bare a son…

A press of air and a deep creaking as the Belgian shifts in his seat. "Can't you hear his briefcase ticking?" The Belgian's breath is sour with Chardonnay and soft cheeses. "Tick-tock. Tick-tock."

And when she saw him that he was a goodly child…

6:42 a.m. Seven hours and fifteen minutes into a seven-hour-forty-minute flight from Chicago to London. Why would 46D wait so long to detonate? The Belgian reads my mind.

"He'll wait until we're over London," he intones. "Ze more casualties, ze better."

She took for him an ark of bulrushes...

I peer out the window. The thinning clouds reveal a patchwork quilt of rich English soil, squares of deep emerald green rising and falling like steady sighs toward the horizon. I long to touch that damp familiar land and inhale the cool fetid loam. But if I die, we'll be together. No. Don't think that. When you reach London, you'll see Cecelia Frost. Just pray: *She took for him an ark of bulrushes, and daubed it with slime and with pitch...*

"Oh my God! Look!" The female voice is garrulously American. 46D stands, clutching his briefcase and caressing the handle.

"It's Candee Cronin!"

Not again.

"Hey, Candee!" The woman barrels toward me, waving a tattered paperback whose cover proclaims: *Assignment: Prague—A Redleigh Smith Mystery.*

The woman stops in the aisle beside me, beaming.

"I'm sorry, but I'm not Candee Cronin," I explain.

The woman—a tall Texan with shellacked hair and oversized silver jewelry—turns the book, revealing a photograph of a thirtysomething woman with bobbed black hair, pale skin, and round blue eyes.

"But Miss Cronin," she protests, indicating the photo, "here y'all are! I'm only like your biggest fan!"

46D, still clutching his briefcase, squeezes past the Texan and stumbles into the aisle.

The woman holds out her heavily jeweled hand. "Audrey Fiscus," she drawls. "It's such an honor. *Assignment: Bangkok* is my all-time favorite. When Redleigh rescues those Green Berets…!"

I shake Audrey's hand as 46D straightens himself and moves toward the restroom. I scan his shoes for exposed wires or a lightable device. "Nice to meet you," I tell Audrey. "But my name is Dayle Salvesen."

Audrey drops my hand and gazes at the paperback, puzzled. "For real? This picture sure looks like you."

I force a smile. "My name is Dayle."

"Sorry." Audrey blushes amiably, but then her eyes narrow. "Unless Dayle is just your alias. Your nom de plume." She shoves the book at the Belgian. "Don't y'all think this is her?"

The Belgian sizes up the photo, then shakes his head. "*Non.* Ze bone structure is not ze same."

46D disappears through the lavatory's folding door. I brace for the explosion, followed by nothing but blue sky for 15,000 feet.

Audrey frowns at the jacket photo. "But check out the eyebrow. There's a little scar right below, and this gal here"— she peers over the Belgian and straight into my face—"has the same little scar."

I pull my battered passport from my backpack and hand it to Audrey. She flips it open and reads: "Surname: Salvesen. Given names: Dayle Anne." Her face falls. "Oh," she says. "Sorry."

"No problem." I take back the passport. "I'm flattered, in fact."

"They're turning her books into a TV series." Audrey brightens. "Starring Hilary Duff."

"So I've heard."

A bell chimes, the seat belt sign blinks on, and a clipped female voice, quintessentially British, comes over the loudspeaker: *Ladies and gentlemen, we're about to begin our initial descent into London Heathrow. Please return to your seats, fasten your seat belts, stow and lock your tray tables, and return your seats to an upright position.*

Audrey squints at me, then rocks back on her heels. "You know, you don't really look much like her at all. Frenchie here is right."

"Oh, well." I return the passport to my backpack. "We can't all be famous authors."

Audrey shuffles back to her seat. Meanwhile, 46D has yet to emerge. Several passengers mass at the lavatory door—a bored teenage girl, a frail elderly man in a fedora, a mother clutching a feisty, red-faced baby. The first casualties, I think bleakly, and return to my prayer: *And she put the child therein; and she laid it in the flags by the river's brink…*

The corpulent Belgian in his creased linen suit reaches into the seat pocket and pulls out the international edition of the *New York Times*. UK TERROR ALERT HIGHEST EVER, the 24-point headline proclaims. AUTHORITIES FEAR ATTACK IS IMMINENT.

The Belgian, sensing me peering over his shoulder, raps the paper with his meaty knuckles. "Frightening, *non*? It won't be much longer now."

Where is 46D? I close my eyes and pray. *And his sister stood afar off, to wit what would be done to him…*

Pressure builds behind my ears as the plane begins its descent. *And the daughter of Pharaoh came down…*

My temples pound. We're so close now. The next twenty minutes will either bring safety, or annihilation.

Ten minutes later a shadow darkens my eyelids. I look up as 46D returns to his seat. Without his briefcase. *Oh no.* I flip open my seat belt and begin to stand. The stewardess rushes down the aisle, briefcase slapping her narrow hip. "Sir?" She is breathless. "You forgot this." She holds out the briefcase and 46D accepts it, blinking a wordless thanks. A dark yoke of sweat spreads from his shoulders to his chest.

A bump, then grinding. *Oh God.* No, it's just the landing gear. 46D rests the briefcase on his lap and fiddles with the locks. Five minutes to touchdown—it will either happen now, or not at all. Just pray: *And the daughter of Pharaoh came down to bathe at the river; and her maidens walked along by the river's side...*

My ears pop. The ambient aircraft noises rush in to fill the void, sounding huge and malevolent.

...and she saw the ark among the flags, and sent her handmaid to fetch it.

The wheels touch ground. Gravity captures the aircraft, drawing me backward and sucking my tailbone deep into the upholstered seat. Buildings, hangars, and other aircraft poised for takeoff shoot past in a blur as we hurtle forward, at one with the earth and all its forces once again. 46D doesn't scare me anymore.

And she opened it, and saw the child: and, behold, the babe wept. "The babe wept," I echo, releasing my fists.

As the plane taxies to the gate, the Belgian grabs my arm with an unexpected intensity. His eyes, formerly a washed-out bluish gray, have turned small and steely in the now more natural light. "Ze flight is over but ze danger remains," he warns. "Safety is only an illusion."

❖

The Belgian's words still ring in my ears as I wait in line at passport control. "What is the nature of your visit?" the officer asks when I reach the front. His ID badge says *Geoffrey Curzon* and he is a thin civil-servant type with a receding hairline and pinched, colorless lips.

"Attending a conference."

"I see." He riffles through my passport. "You've spent a great deal of time in the UK."

"Yes."

"Over the course of several years." He licks a fingertip, then pages through my passport again, this time in reverse.

"Yes." The strap of my laptop bag presses heavily against my neck.

"Conference, you say?"

"That's right. I'm giving the keynote speech." I pull a small white envelope from my backpack and place it on the countertop.

Curzon opens the envelope, takes out the invitation, and types something into his computer. His eyebrows arch as his pupils collapse to tiny slits.

"Please come with me, Miss Salvesen."

"Why?"

"Just come with me." He steps down from his stool and around his glass-sided pod. Clutching my arm, he leads me out of passport control, through a bank of elevators, and down a long, narrow, darkened hallway. He opens a door, one of several in a row, and guides me into a small, windowless room with bare white walls, two metal chairs, and a clear Plexiglas table. Another man, already inside and leaning, arms folded, against the far wall, motions for me to drop my bags and extend my arms. The heavyset fellow steps closer, waves an electronic wand over me, then starts to pat me down. My eye is level with his ID badge, which reads *Barry Everton*.

"I'd prefer a female officer," I say carefully.

Everton's bloodshot eyes retract into the folds of his fleshy face. "If you insist. But it might be a while."

"All right then." I sigh and lift my arms again, just wanting to get this over. No doubt Celia is already waiting for me in the arrivals area. I can just see her, clutching an unlit cigarette, with her hair disheveled and day-old mascara smeared across her cheek. She is defiantly beautiful as she slouches, tapping her foot.

Everton's plump, stubby hands are lewd and brutish, lingering at my breasts and cupping my butt. I fight back tears.

"Take a seat," Everton orders, pointing to one of the small metal chairs. Geoffrey Curzon flips the invitation onto the table. "This is for a Candee Cronin," he says as I sit down.

"Yes. That's my pseudonym."

No response.

"You know—my pen name."

Curzon and Everton exchange glances without saying a word.

Nervous, I continue. "I'm speaking on Contemporary Genre Fiction and the Post-Feminist Paradigm. I'll be explaining how, by embracing seemingly stereotypical female pursuits such as shopping and romance, our protagonists are in fact creating a new, and ultimately empowering, feminist norm."

Everton grabs the other chair and straddles it, pressing his weight against the table. The thin, efficient Curzon, still standing, picks up my passport and cracks it open, bending back the cover. He licks his index finger and pages through it, nodding. I know what he sees: Bangkok, Jakarta, Hamburg...

"Miss Cronin..."

"My name is Dayle Salvesen."

"Miss Cronin, did you travel to Madrid on the fifteenth of January this year?"

Madrid? "Yes. For the book fair."

"And did you travel from Munich to Budapest on the second of February?"

"Yes. For a literary festival." My voice quivers. "Look, call my agent in New York. Call the conference organizers here in London. I'm sure we can sort this out."

I'm interrupted by a knock at the door. "Come," Everton barks. A young woman in uniform enters. She could have frisked me. She hands Everton a folded piece of paper, whispers in his ear, and quickly retreats. Everton leans forward. His meaty forearms flatten on the table, looking as pink and greasy as boiled hams.

"Miss Cronin, I'm afraid you won't be allowed to enter the UK today."

"Why not?" My head spins.

"Your name is on the terrorist watch list."

CHAPTER TWO

Wednesday
7:54 a.m.

Everton slaps the paper on the table in front of me. It's a photocopied mug shot of a young, dark-haired woman with a hard-set mouth and pale, penetrating eyes.

"Candace Marie Cronin. Age thirty-four. Known IRA associate. Born in Dublin but travels on an American passport," Everton recites.

"So?"

"Arrested two years ago in Madrid. Served six months in Holloway prison."

I glance at the photo again and make the connection. "You think that's *me*?"

"Can't deny the resemblance."

"But I'm really a blonde," I say, then realize that Terrorist Candace might be naturally blond too. "Look, you've got my passport. I am Dayle Anne Salvesen, born in Green Bay, Wisconsin, on February 17th, 1978, to Sven and Katherine Salvesen."

"Tell us again why you are here."

"For the Women and Fiction conference. It's tonight at Dartmouth House, sponsored by The English-Speaking Union. I'm giving the keynote speech."

"I see. And why do you continue returning to the UK?"

"Because I *like* the place?"

Everton is not amused. "We've called for our supervisor," he warns.

"Good." I cross my arms and try to sound brave. "He'll see that I'm Dayle Salvesen." I am aware that beneath their polite and deferential exteriors, the British are tough customers. How worried should I be?

"Whom will you visit during your stay?" Curzon asks, pacing behind Everton.

"You want their names?" My voice cracks. The British devised the infamous so-called five techniques of interrogation during Operation Demetrius in Northern Ireland in the early 1970s.

"Yes, their names," Everton growls.

The five techniques of interrogation are wall standing, hooding, noise bombardment, sleep deprivation, and deprivation of food and water. I doubt I could survive any one of them, much less all five.

"Names? There's so many." I stall. Instinctively I want to protect Cecelia. From what, I do not know. "I first lived in the UK as an exchange student in high school. Then study abroad, junior year of college. I did my MA in Norwich and lived in London for two years after that. I must know hundreds of Britons."

"Why do you possess this invitation for Candee Cronin?"

"I told you—that's my pen name." My fictional heroine, Redleigh Smith, is a C-level graduate of the US military's

SERE program: Survival, Evasion, Resistance, Escape. Neither Redleigh nor I will go down without a fight.

"Something wrong with your real name?" Curzon poses.

"If Dayle Salvesen *is* your real name," Everton taunts.

"It's complicated," I say evasively. What do they actually do to people in these situations? Torture? Waterboarding? They don't *really* think I'm a terrorist, do they?

"We've got time," Curzon offers.

"All the time in the world," Everton adds.

I sit forward, place my palms on the cool Plexiglas table, and take a deep breath before speaking. "My publisher suggested I use a new name when I started writing thrillers." I don't reveal that, in fact, I *had* to use a pseudonym—my Dayle Salvesen books sold so poorly I was told I would never be published again, except as someone else.

"Why Candee Cronin?"

I shake my head, maintaining eye contact. I must stay strong; they will exploit any sign of weakness. "No reason. Had I known about Candace Marie Cronin, I'd have picked something else." Will they at least let me call a lawyer? What will my family be told?

A staccato knock rattles the door behind me. Startled, I jump. Everton eyes me icily. "Anything else you'd like to tell us?"

"No."

Curzon opens the door. The supervisor enters and she is not what I expected. Early fifties, she is five foot six and slim, in a crisp navy-blue suit with long auburn hair wound in a bun and minimal makeup on her translucent skin. Pressed to her hip is a hardcover copy of *Assignment: Sao Paulo*, published six weeks ago. Peeking from between the pages of the book is a receipt, indicating that the book was purchased from an airport bookshop just minutes ago.

"It *is* you!" she exclaims, scanning my face.

"Ma'am?" the men ask, confused.

The woman steps to my side and extends her hand. "Laura Winchester," she says. "Pleased to meet you."

"Thank you. I'm Dayle Salvesen," I reply as we shake. "Also known as Candee Cronin."

"Miss Cronin! I'm a big fan of your books." She settles into the chair across from me and smiles.

Curzon and Everton, now standing shoulder to shoulder, look away like schoolboys rebuked. "Ma'am, we were concerned this woman could be Candace Marie Cronin." Curzon hands her the photocopied mug shot.

Winchester leans forward and squints, pursing her lips. "There is a resemblance, I'll grant." She places the mug shot next to the book's back jacket, the majority of which is taken up by my publicity photo. To see the images side by side is striking: the alleged IRA terrorist and I could be long-lost sisters. And it is especially strange that we employ such similar names.

"But the woman in this photo"—Winchester taps the book jacket—"has a small scar just below the left eyebrow. The woman in the other photo does not."

I slide my hand up my forehead, lifting my bangs. "That's me. See? Here's the scar."

Winchester cranes across the table and stares at my eyebrow, then settles back in her seat, satisfied. "Yes, indeed. Chaps, we have before us the author Candee Cronin, not the terrorist Candace Marie."

Apparently satisfied, Curzon and Everton tell me I'm free to go. As I gather up my things, Winchester slips a ballpoint pen from her jacket pocket and places it on the table beside the book. "You will sign this for me, of course?"

"Sure." My hand trembles as I take the pen. "Should I make it out to…?"

"Laura is fine." She smiles, tucking a loose strand of auburn hair behind her ear. "Can't wait to read it. Hope it's as good as *Assignment: Bangkok.*"

When I finish I hand the book back to her and she touches my elbow. "Do be careful during your visit," she warns with a frown. "We're in the midst of a major security alert."

I am still shaking following my interrogation as I collect my suitcase from baggage claim, pass through customs, and emerge into the arrivals area, which is packed with all manner of humanity. I search the scores of faces for Cecelia Frost, for the familiar features that will resemble my own. Celia is the bad-girl version of me, edgy in every way I am not: wry, stylish, and bold. Friends since our teens and briefly lovers, we were stars of the famed creative writing program at England's University of East Anglia six years ago. It is remarkable to think how dramatically both our lives have changed since then, my life in one direction and hers in another.

Can you believe they thought I was an IRA terrorist? Saved by the little scar below my eyebrow. In my mind I'm busy spinning the story for Celia, making it funnier and more dramatic. Worthy of her hearing.

After searching for several minutes with no luck, I pull out my cell phone and call Celia. After several rings I hear a click followed by her familiar Oxbridge accent: *Hello. You have reached the London Refugee Relief Centre. Please leave a message and someone will return your call as soon as possible.*

I scan the concourse as I speak. "Celia, it's Dayle. I'm still at Heathrow. If you get this message, stay put. I'll be there soon."

I regret the message as soon as I hang up. I should have been sharper, wittier. More like Celia.

❖

Just outside the arrivals area, awash in a cold, drab sea of rain-darkened concrete, is a taxi stand. I grab the first black cab in the queue and settle in for the fifty-minute journey to Hampstead. My driver is an old-school East Ender, thick necked and tattooed, with crooked yellow teeth. The fatigue of the long flight and subsequent questioning creeps up on me as the soft patter of rain lulls me toward sleep.

Traffic is slow and heavy, as always, and I struggle to stay awake as we pass through the uninspired suburbs with their ribbons of run-down row houses and abandoned industrial estates that line the motorway from Heathrow eastward into the city. I last lived in London four years ago and haven't even been back to visit in the last year and a half, but nothing much has changed. The city always seems to be under construction; as soon as one project is done, something right next door gets under way. London never feels finished to me; it's as if someone parted the curtains and unlocked the door before the shop was ready to open, and now the city is trapped in an endless cycle, struggling to catch up.

The taxi's radio drones softly in the background, barely audible, until an announcer breaks in with a news bulletin and the driver raises the volume: *The capital is on high alert as Britain's home secretary today warned Londoners to remain vigilant in the face of what has been described as the very real threat of a major terrorist attack...* The driver turns down the sound.

"You a Yank?" he asks suddenly, glaring darkly at me in the rearview mirror.

"Yes," I reply.

"It figures," he scoffs.

"I'm sorry?"

"We have Iraq, Afghanistan, and you lot to thank for this mess."

❖

I stir to life as we enter Hampstead, which, despite the low slate-colored late-March sky, appears as leafy and prosperous as a well-heeled Victorian resort, with old-fashioned pubs, trendy restaurants, and expensive designer shops. People spill from the Hampstead Tube stop onto the cobblestone sidewalk, dodging raindrops and rushing into elegant cafés while avoiding the outdoor seating arranged beneath broad, wind-battered canopies.

At least Celia lives in a nice neighborhood, I think, as we wind southward down the hill through bumper-to-bumper traffic. I know she has struggled recently, personally and professionally, and I haven't been the most attentive friend.

"Number ten, Rosslyn Hill," the cab driver announces as we squeal to a sudden stop in front of a ragged Victorian mansion, several stories high and showing serious signs of decay. Leave it to Celia to choose the only tumbledown structure marooned amidst a sea of luxury.

I grab my luggage, step outside, and reach into my backpack to pay the driver.

"Word in your ear, love," he says as I give him four twenty-pound notes and a tenner.

"What's that?" I crouch to see him through the opened window.

He scowls. "Best pretend you're Canadian, at least for the next few days."

As the cab eases back into traffic, I haul my suitcase up the crumbling concrete steps to the building's massive front door, painted strangely pink within the otherwise cream-white exterior and edged on either side with panels of smoke-damaged stained glass. I ring the buzzer for flat number five. No answer. I ring again. Still no answer, so I nudge the door with my shoulder and it inches open into a dimly lit lobby with a split staircase rising to the upper floors. One hundred years ago this would have been an elegant one-family mansion, but now, monumentally disheveled, it resembles an elderly lady whose regal bearing retains only faint traces of her perfumed youth.

I ascend to the second floor, where a rank odor seeps into the darkened hallway, a combination of rust, cooking fat, and excrement. I find the door with the numeral 5 hanging loosely from a nail and lift my hand to knock, but the door swings open at my touch.

"Celia?" My voice sounds as tired as I feel.

Celia's apartment is cold, damp, and tiny, a single rectangular room, every inch of which is immediately visible. I drop my luggage and gaze around the haphazard mess. There's a single bed, consisting of two flabby mattresses stacked one atop the other, without a box spring or frame. One corner of the room contains a chest of drawers and a warped wooden wardrobe with layers of clothing draped over the door; the opposite wall features a card-table desk with a telephone, answering machine, computer, printer, and fax, barely visible between teetering towers of paper. From this modest office, Celia single-handedly runs The London Refugee Relief Centre, through which she organizes support and resources for refugees, asylum seekers, and modern-day sex slaves from around the world who seek safety and sanctuary in the UK.

Across the room is the kitchenette with a spider-veined sink stained copper and green, a dorm-size fridge, and a combination hot plate/toaster oven, covered with what looks like congealed cheese. Balanced on a shelf above the sink are a CD player, scattered CDs, several overflowing ashtrays, and a small TV. The mold-infested bathroom contains a toilet, sink, and tub.

I imagine Celia will be back soon and left the door unlocked for me. Giving in to exhaustion, I take off my coat, lie down on Celia's double mattresses, and sink almost to the floor. Loose coils poke my elbows while the familiar, heady scent of Celia—a mixture of cigarettes, sweaty feet, and Ryvita crackers—rings my head. I settle into the bed's remembered dimensions of her body: narrow trenches for limbs, and the hollow that nightly cradles her skull, a skull that once nestled so expertly in the warm palm of my hand.

From where I lie I can see Celia's desk and copies of both of our first books: my novel—Dayle Salvesen's novel—*Down on Euclid Avenue*, and Celia's acclaimed collection of short stories, *West of Blessing, North of Hope*. Beside the books are framed photos, one of Celia with a tall, square-shouldered biracial woman who must be the girlfriend I've yet to meet, Edwina Adebayo. Another shows Celia and me in our undergraduate days, round-cheeked and eager, dressed in jeans and matching sweatshirts. The third photograph is a faded color print, creased down the middle, of a gaunt, middle-aged woman, head in a kerchief, sitting on a bench beneath Blackpool Tower and cradling an overdressed infant.

Curious, I rise from the mattress, reach over, and take the photo, removing it from its frame. On the back someone has scrawled: *Maggie + Celia. Oct. '78.* Of course. Celia and her mother. This would have been less than three years before Maggie died. I realize, in the twenty-plus years I have known Celia, this is the first I've seen a picture of her mother.

I replace the photo and lie back down, linking my fingers behind my head. I look at the walls, where the flocked velvet wallpaper has peeled off in strips, exposing ancient gray brickwork beneath. The only decorations are two posters, one from the International Campaign to Ban Landmines, the other from Amnesty International's 1981 fund-raiser, The Secret Policeman's Other Ball.

So it's come to this, I think sadly. Six years ago, Celia shone with literary promise, brimming with a fluid and natural gift; now she's reduced to living in what the British call a bedsit. My condo on Chicago's Lake Shore Drive has closets bigger than Celia's apartment.

After Celia phoned in December and invited me to visit, I did some research and discovered that her last book was savaged by critics, and the publisher canceled the second in her two-book deal. But she's doing the work of a Lord she has never believed in, every day delivering desperate souls to safety. Writing fiction must seem small, compared to that.

Suddenly there's a noise in the corridor. *Celia?* I sit up quickly and my head spins. I must have drifted off to sleep. Dizzy, I clutch the mattress and my fingers sink into the cotton batting.

"Hello? Is someone there?" a voice calls meekly from the hall.

"Yes. In here," I reply.

An elderly woman appears in the doorway, nervously rubbing her hands. She is small and sinewy, dressed in an oversize housecoat and ragged slippers. "Oh, I didn't know you'd arrived—"

"It's okay." I want to stand but fatigue keeps me glued to the makeshift bed. "My name is Dayle Salvesen and—"

"Oh, I know who you are." She pauses. "I'm so sorry, love. Cecelia Frost is dead."

CHAPTER THREE

Wednesday
9:35 a.m.

"Come along, now. Wake up, love."

Someone pats my hand rapidly and breathes into my face. My vision has blackened; I'm spinning into a dark hole without dimension, without end.

"There's a good girl. Eh? Let's get you some tea."

My vision clears. The woman looms over me, tipped forward with fists on hips.

"Tea?" I whisper. "All right."

The woman takes my elbow and helps up me from the Celia-scented mattress. Celia's ghostly odor rises with me, dissipates, then disappears. Dumbly I follow the woman out of Celia's flat and down the hall past two other flats to her own. Although no bigger than Celia's, this room is painted canary yellow, with pressed lace curtains and a box of ambitiously British flowers, stiff stemmed and stubbornly colored, gracing the windowsill.

"Here we are, love. Have a little rest." The woman sits me down at the table and putters in her kitchenette, switching on the electric kettle and opening a small tin of tea bags. Across the room she has a twin bed with a quilted duvet, upon which rests a listless tabby cat, sleepily eying a caged budgerigar.

"I'm sorry, Mrs....?" My voice cracks. "I don't know your name."

"Dolores Crawford," she answers proudly. "Friends call me Dot."

"Dot." I draw a deep breath. "Celia died?"

She nods solemnly. "'Fraid so."

"When?"

"Early this morning."

"How?"

She taps her foot, waiting for the kettle to boil. "I don't know the whole story, mind you. The police only left a quarter hour ago." As the water heats, so does Dot's excitement. "Apparently they found Celia's car near Waterloo Bridge. They reckon she jumped."

"Have they found her body?"

"They didn't say."

"So she might still be alive." Hope. I have hope. A car is not a body.

Dot turns from the sink and considers me with pity. "Well, Celia's had some...troubles," she says gently.

"Troubles?"

"Yes. She tried to off herself." Dot pauses dramatically. "Twice."

"What?"

"Oh yes." Suddenly animated, Dot can't wait to share the sordid tale. "First time must have been 'round about a year ago. She done slit her wrists. It was only her girlfriend getting her to hospital in time that saved her life."

"And the second time?"

Dot scowls, searching her memory. "Two months ago? Overdosed on sleeping tablets. Again the girlfriend rescued her. Reckon this time, she couldn't help."

"Why not?"

"They ended it two weeks ago." The kettle clicks off and Dot pours the boiling water over tea bags in two mismatched ceramic mugs. She fingers their cracked handles, waiting for the tea to brew.

"I don't understand." I shake my head. "We'd been out of touch for a while, but when Celia phoned me before Christmas, she seemed fine."

"Maybe she was ashamed...?" Dot looks down at her well-worn slippers.

"Ashamed of what?"

"Well, I shouldn't be telling stories out of school, but money was tight. The landlord was always pestering her for the rent and Celia was always pleading, *Just a few more days, sir, just a few more days.*"

Dot removes the tea bags and balances them beside the sink, from where I imagine she will use them later, squeezing out the last few drops of a thin and bitter liquid.

"Then, last week, Celia was attacked in the street," Dot continues, placing a pint of milk on the table and setting down the mugs. *In Celebration of The Royal Wedding, HRH Prince Charles and Lady Diana, 29th July 1981*, my mug proclaims in fancy lettering, while the royal couple stare straight ahead and smile brightly, unaware of their sad future.

"Celia was attacked?" I ask.

"Yes. She came home with a black eye and a gashed cheek. Said someone grabbed her handbag and she fought back. She was a bit woozy, so I did the neighborly thing and cleaned her up"—Dot nods over her shoulder—"with that very tea towel. Haven't done my washing yet."

I glance at the threadbare towel's brownish, *S*-shaped smear of blood. Celia's blood, still visible. Like Celia's scent, still trapped in her mattress. How can she have died? So much of her remains.

I sip the tea, cradling the hot liquid in my throat. "I knew Celia had some problems, but nothing…" Suddenly I stop and listen: steady footsteps climb the staircase and turn toward Celia's flat. "Should your neighbors be home now?"

Dot shrugs. "Colonel Fielding doesn't get out much anymore. The amputation and all. Why?"

"Come with me." I set down the mug and beckon Dot to follow. She is officially having the most exciting day of her life. I hold my finger to my lips and tiptoe, motioning for silence.

We creep down the hallway, past the staircase and toward Celia's flat. The door is open, but not enough to see in. Someone is opening and closing drawers, searching, rustling. I push the door and it flies open, banging against the wall.

A woman standing at the dresser jumps back and gasps as the drawer she'd been holding clatters to the floor. She is in her early forties, tall and thin with a long, narrow face, beaky nose, and lank dirty-blond hair.

"DC Callaway?" Dot asks, surprised. "I thought you'd finished here."

The woman smoothes her dark blue skirt and peels off her rubber gloves. "Yes…well, I was. But I wanted to double-check something."

"Oh. This is Cecelia's friend from the States…?" Dot searches for my name.

"Dayle Salvesen," I say, extending my hand as Dot and I step closer. Callaway's hand as she takes mine feels cold and lifeless. She strikes me as a peevish, impatient woman who probably smokes and is prone to being judgmental.

"Detective Constable Andrea Callaway," she says briskly, picking up the drawer she'd dropped and forcing it back into the dresser. "Metropolitan Police. Sorry about your friend."

"Have you found her body?" I ask, swallowing hard.

She shakes her head. "No. Not yet. But that's not surprising. The way the river flows, she could be out to sea by now."

I envision the Thames, snaking sluggishly around the boroughs of London and flushing into the North Sea, belching more than 200 miles worth of waste and detritus into the cold murky waters. Celia deserves better than that.

"Dayle doesn't believe Cecelia offed herself," Dot volunteers.

"I understand. But she left a note—a suicide note—in the vehicle." Callaway grimaces. "Regarding next of kin...?"

"There isn't any," I say sadly. "Celia was an only child. Her mother died when she was three and her father last year. Someone will have to tell her girlfriend. *Ex*-girlfriend? And those orphans..."

"Orphans?" Both Dot and the detective look confused.

"Refugees. Those people she helps. How will they survive without her?" Suddenly I feel faint.

Dot and Callaway help me into a chair. Celia's chair. "There, there, love," Dot comforts. "You've had quite a shock."

Callaway fills a glass with water from the sink and brings it to me. I drink gratefully from the rim stained by Celia's lips.

"I'd like to speak with you about Ms. Frost, later, when you're feeling better. Attempt to establish her mental state." Callaway hands me her card. "Where are you staying?"

I look around the tiny flat. "Here? With Celia." That sounds impossible now. "I'll get a hotel. I'm speaking at a conference tonight." I sigh. "I don't know."

"Have a little rest at my place, then decide," Dot offers.

She is beyond generous, but suddenly I have to be alone. "Thanks, but I think I'll stay here," I say. "Try to collect myself."

"All right then, but I'm just down the corridor if you need me." Dot pats my shoulder.

Callaway nods at the card still in my hand. "My number's there, if you think of anything that could be useful to the investigation. I'm at the Hampstead police station just up the road—twenty-six Rosslyn Hill."

"Of course. I'll let you know." I walk Dot and Callaway to the door and bid them good-bye. Once they have gone, the silence inside the little flat is deafening. I quickly phone the airline and change my ticket. I had planned to stay in London for ten days, but instead I book a flight back to Chicago for early tomorrow afternoon. I'm sure there will be a funeral, paperwork to complete, a whole life needing to be dismantled, but I can't be any part of that. Celia would understand. It's too soon after Rory.

I sit at Celia's desk and press my palms to my face. *Could Celia have killed herself?* I consider the facts: Celia's only family, her father, died a year ago. She had serious financial problems. Her last book was a critical and commercial failure. Dot says Celia attempted suicide twice in the past year. She recently broke up with her girlfriend. A few days ago, she was mugged. Enough to make someone depressed, no doubt. But suicidal? Celia knew I was arriving today. Couldn't she have waited? Was she afraid I'd try to talk her out of it? Wasn't our friendship of more than twenty years worth at least a final good-bye?

I pace the tiny apartment. There are things here that don't make sense: dirty dishes fill the sink, but Celia's fridge is almost empty, as if she'd cleared out all the food. A brand-new suitcase, price tag still on it, sits inside the wooden wardrobe with a stack of clean clothes folded neatly on top. On her desk, maps of Dublin and of the DART, Dublin's rail line. A box of black hair dye, in a plastic bag with a receipt. Purchased four days ago, with cash. I'm convinced Celia planned to return to this flat. Return, then leave forever.

I go into the bathroom and wash my hands. While I search for a clean towel in the wooden shelves beneath the sink, something catches my eye. Pushing aside some linens I pull out what looks like a brand-new credit card. It's in the name of Marguerite Alderton and signed with a flowery signature. Was Celia desperate enough to steal someone's credit card?

The phone rings and I jump. My hands are shaking as I pick up the phone and say hello.

"Oh, hello." The deep voice pauses. "Celia?"

"No. Dayle Salvesen."

"Oh, right—Celia's friend from the States. May I speak to Celia?"

"Is this Edwina Adebayo?" I think I recognize a slight West African accent.

"Why, yes it is."

"Edwina, I don't know how to tell you this. Celia died this morning."

She gasps. "That's not possible."

"I didn't think so either. But the police were just here—"

"No, I mean it isn't *possible*," Edwina interrupts. "Celia rang me five minutes ago."

CHAPTER FOUR

Wednesday
10:19 a.m.

"You talked to Celia? She's alive?" My mind races. I'm angry with Dot Crawford for letting me think that Celia had died. It's all Dot's fault, and I am thrilled and enlivened to have someone to blame.

"I didn't speak to her, no." Edwina's voice is thin and nervous. My heart tumbles. "My mobile rang," she continues quickly. "No one was there when I answered, but the number on the screen was Celia's."

Hatred for Dot Crawford creeps back into my consciousness. But Celia might be alive; perhaps she was calling for help.

"Look, I'm just down the road," Edwina says. "Stay where you are and I'll be right there."

"Okay," I manage to reply. "Please hurry."

I hang up the phone, and while I wait for Edwina I search Celia's flat again, wondering what I'm missing. I think about Redleigh Smith, my alter ego; actually, my alter ego's alter ego, since I, Dayle Salvesen, write as Candee Cronin, and Candee Cronin, whom I did not know until this morning was an aspiring terrorist, created Redleigh Smith, heroine of the

Assignment novels. Redleigh always knows what to do and looks good in a bikini while doing it. She carries truth serum in a lipstick tube and once strangled two al-Qaeda operatives with her thong.

Celia's tiny flat is dense with dirty clothes, notes scribbled on paper napkins, greasy Chinese takeout containers, and makeshift ashtrays. I have no idea what I'm looking for as I shift haphazard piles of papers and gather loose shoes. In the bottom drawer of Celia's desk I find a sealed manila envelope labeled *Personal Documents*. I'm not ready to open it, at least not yet. Then I notice a gap of several inches between Celia's stacked mattresses and the wall. Kneeling on the bed, I slide my hand into the space and move forward until I hit something.

It's a new cell phone, still in its box, although the box has been opened. Inside the box, stashed beneath the phone, is a large wad of twenty- and fifty-pound notes. Counting it quickly, it comes to over £5,000 pounds—more than $7,500 dollars. What the hell? I turn on the phone and by its prefix I can tell the number's not British.

A knock at the door startles me. I quickly stuff the items back behind the mattress. "Come in," I call loudly.

The door opens slowly and standing in the darkened doorway is a gorgeous square-shouldered woman in her late thirties, about six feet tall, with loose black curls clipped close above her ears and at the nape of her long, elegant neck. Her cocoa-colored skin is smooth and flawless, unadorned by makeup, and she has surprisingly pale gray eyes. Her high cheekbones and wide forehead give her face an open and inviting quality. She is dressed in a powder-blue button-down Oxford shirt, straight-leg jeans, a black leather bomber jacket and black Dr. Martens boots.

"Hello, I'm Edwina Adebayo," she says softly.

I step across the room and extend my hand. "Dayle Salvesen," I say. "Pleased to meet you. I only wish the circumstances were different."

As we shake, her muscular hand is clammy and trembling. "Celia's mobile. When she was robbed...her purse..."

"I know." I guide Edwina to a chair. "I thought of that too, right after you called. Was Celia's cell phone in her purse when she was mugged?"

Edwina shakes her head. "I really couldn't say."

"It's possible that whoever called you just now has Celia's phone and simply punched in your preset number."

"It's possible." Edwina takes a deep breath and swallows, looking up at me with vacant gray eyes. "Do you believe Celia is dead?"

I shake my head. "I honestly don't know. The police think so. They found her car, and a suicide note, near Waterloo Bridge this morning. But they haven't found a body."

Edwina's eyes fill with tears. "She's gone and done it this time," she whispers bitterly. "It's my fault. I should have been here."

I place my hand on her shoulder and feel the strong muscles shift beneath my fingertips. "Don't blame yourself," I say, then remember how often I was told the same thing myself, five months ago. "If Celia wanted to die, no one could have saved her."

Edwina blinks rapidly and draws a breath. As she glances around the flat, I imagine what she sees: places where she and Celia laughed and cuddled, made dinner and watched TV, and places even more intimate—Celia's underwear drawer, the bathtub, the bed where they made love.

"Let's get out of here," I whisper. "Fresh air will do us both good."

She nods, swiping her eyes with her thumbs. "Are you hungry?"

The question seems so preposterous, I laugh out loud. How could I eat now? And yet I am hungry—famished, in fact. I haven't had a decent meal since before my flight left Chicago yesterday evening. "Starving," I reply.

"Come on then. There's a nice place just up the road."

We leave Celia's flat and, fighting the blustery wind and scattershot rain, head north up Rosslyn Hill, past trendy boutiques, tall red-brick town houses, and elegant cafés. The affluent, sophisticated feel of the neighborhood stands in stark contrast to the squalor of Celia's flat.

Edwina steps briskly in her heavy boots and I struggle to keep pace with her long, determined strides. We are silent, except for our quickening breath, as we proceed uphill, and in the silence I observe Edwina—tall, confident, powerful—from the corner of my eye. So this is—this was?—Celia's partner. I am surprised; most of Celia's girlfriends, other than me, have been delicate, ethereal waifs with soft, feminine features.

"Tell me about Celia's recent work," I ask, glancing at Edwina as we stop to cross Willoughby Road and are nearly mowed down by a frantic Mini Cooper. "We've been out of touch the past several months."

"Well, for a start, she's made some changes at the center."

"What kind of changes?"

"She no longer works primarily with asylum seekers and refugees, as she did before." Edwina plunges her hands into her jacket pockets as we resume walking. "Now Celia deals almost exclusively with young women and girls—mainly from Asia and Eastern Europe—who have been trafficked into Britain as sex slaves and child prostitutes. She helps get them off the streets and into group homes, foster care, or sheltered accommodation."

"Sounds challenging," I offer, pleased that Edwina's gait has slowed enough that my shorter strides keep pace with hers. The sidewalk seems to narrow as we maneuver past a frumpy, frazzled mum pushing a double stroller.

"More challenging than you might imagine," Edwina muses, blinking against the wind. "Celia doesn't just shuffle papers and answer phones. She's committed to working on the ground as well. Last year she sneaked into Moldova on the back of a lorry with a group of aid workers, hoping to document the circumstances there."

"Sounds like the kind of work where she might make enemies."

Edwina stubs her boot on a broken paving stone and I clutch her arm so she doesn't tumble.

"You think it's foul play?" she asks, leaning against me as she finds her footing, tapping the toe of one boot with the heel of the other.

"I have no idea," I admit. "I'm just not convinced Celia would kill herself."

Edwina straightens and looks away uneasily.

"What is it?" I ask.

"Celia attempted suicide," she whispers, as if to cushion the blow. "Twice, in fact, in the past year. About two months ago she overdosed on sleeping tablets and ended up in hospital."

I hunch my shoulders to fight off the cold. "I know. Celia's neighbor, Dot, mentioned that to me. But I'm still not convinced."

"There is something else." Edwina frowns, biting her lip. "What?"

"I don't believe the mugging was a random street crime, as Celia claimed. I think it was a warning to back off, or else."

I knew there was more to the story. "Had she received any specific threats?" I ask.

Edwina shakes her head. "None that I know of, but we spoke less frequently since we split up."

"But the breakup was amicable?"

"Yes…" She looks away.

"But?" I'm hesitant to push too hard.

The rising wind teases tears from Edwina's eyes. "I'm not even certain *why* we broke up, truth be told. We had been very happy—at least I was and believed she was as well. Then about a month ago, she became distant. Secretive." A shadow darkens her face.

"Was there someone else?" I ask carefully.

She tucks her chin to her chest and resumes walking, at a pace even brisker than before. "I don't believe so. She said she needed space and we should separate. I tried changing her mind, but she was adamant. And you know how Celia is, once she sets her mind to something."

Boy, did I know. But I felt a strange stab of remorse that someone knew Celia as well as, or better than, I once had. When we were lovers, I foolishly believed that we knew one another better than any two people ever could—the ultimate fallacy of love.

We reach the café, a cheerful French bistro called Au Bon Tartine, with the day's specials scrawled in rain-smudged chalk on a blackboard propped against the open door. Edwina guides me inside the noisy café, which is surprisingly busy for just before eleven a.m. on a Wednesday morning. We take a small marble table facing the foggy front window, where we can observe the thick traffic lumbering up Hampstead High Street, belching dense clouds of exhaust that hang heavily, skirting the pavement like old-fashioned crinolines.

We order Diet Cokes, salade Niçoise, and share a plate of *pommes frites*. The food is fresh and delicious and I realize how truly hungry I was.

"So you're the famous author." Edwina reveals a slightly gap-toothed grin as she sips her Diet Coke. "Celia lent me *Assignment: Colombia*. I loved when your heroine broke up the drug cartel."

"Yes. By replacing several hundred kilos of cocaine with talcum powder and flying the real stuff back to Miami in a hijacked Cessna 182 Skylane." I feel myself blush. "My novels are nothing but superficial escapism, devoured by straight suburban soccer moms."

Her eyebrows rise. "And yet you continue writing them."

Her challenge surprises me but I try to shrug it off. "I was a serious writer, until my agent suggested I do a thriller for a new publishing house in the States. Next I knew, they said yes and I was earning more in six months than I had in my lifetime."

Edwina looks surprised and takes a moment to dab her lip with the napkin before responding. "Surely you no longer need the money."

"True. But now I'm in too deep—contracted for three more books." I pause, watching beads of condensation merge and trickle down the ghostly glass window. "I sometimes think I lost Celia's respect. When we were young and struggling, we swore we'd never sell out. We'd maintain our commitment to literature, or some such thing. But now, not only am I pandering to commercial concerns, I'm writing books that are straighter than straight, full of glamour and hetero romance."

"Cecelia wouldn't have minded such success." Edwina very deliberately saws into a green bean, then pushes an anchovy to the side of her plate.

"Maybe not." I pick up a french fry and swipe it through the salad's vinaigrette. "But she would have used the money to help refugees and the underprivileged. I, on the other hand, bought a BMW and a lakefront condo."

Edwina puts down her fork and looks me straight in the eye. "Celia thinks the world of you," she insists. "She's always going on about Dayle, the best-selling author, and how proud she is of you."

"Oh." I don't know what to say. The truth is that I have barely even thought about Celia over the past six months, my mind so preoccupied with other things.

As Edwina and I continue to eat in silence, occasionally glancing up to watch traffic, I think back to first meeting Celia when we were both thirteen and she and her father arrived in Green Bay on his Fulbright fellowship. Celia, with her black leather, her Mohawk, and her multiple piercings, touched down like a tornado. She listened to The Smiths, Pixies, Fields of the Nephilim; had friends back home airmailing her copies of *New Musical Express*. Celia introduced me to Anaïs Nin, Henry Miller, Sylvia Plath, and *Lady Chatterley's Lover* while our school library was banning Judy Blume's *Are You There God? It's Me, Margaret*. The world became infinitely larger and more interesting the moment I first laid eyes upon Cecelia Frost.

"How did you and Celia meet?" I ask Edwina softly, breaking the silent spell.

Edwina's eyes ignite as she glances up from her salad. "It was at a charity reading to raise money for a church in Nigeria," she explains. "I have a vested interest—I was born in Lagos to a Nigerian father and a mother from Devon." The gap-toothed smile briefly reappears. "The reading was at Persephone, and Celia read that scene from *West of Blessing*—you know, the bee-sting scene." She sighs. "Love at first sight."

"Sounds wonderful."

"More than wonderful. Life altering." Edwina smiles sadly, then glances at her watch, a large silver Breitling, a man's watch that makes her broad hand and wrist look narrower and more feminine. "Oh, it's twenty past. I must go—I've a lecture at one." She rises from her chair and slips a worn leather wallet from her back pocket, then pulls out a business card and hands it to me. It says *Edwina Adebayo— Junior Lecturer, Department of English, University of London*, above her address and phone number. "Ring me if you hear anything. *Anything*," she emphasizes, plunging her arms into her jacket and hefting it over her shoulders. Her generous bottom lip trembles as her large round eyes revert to a troubled shade of pastel gray. "Please find my Celia. Tell me that she's all right."

I slip the card into my backpack. "Believe me—I'll do everything I can."

We leave the café and after saying our good-byes, Edwina heads north to the Tube station while I turn and head south, back to Celia's flat. Dot Crawford is still buzzing with excitement as I greet her in the building's decrepit front lobby.

"DC Callaway spoke to me for *ages* after we left you," she says proudly. Dot has changed into a dark skirt, white blouse, and gray cardigan with white support hose and sensible shoes. I imagine she is waiting for a ride as she busily plays with the clasp on her handbag. "And she may even need to interview me *again*!"

"I'm sure you've been very helpful," I reply, smiling in spite of myself.

I make my way up the darkened, foul-smelling staircase and enter Celia's unlocked flat, which assaults me with its emptiness, its gaping silence, its utter lack of Celia. Celia was a physical entity, alive and present, while Edwina and I spoke. But now Celia has vanished, disappeared, retreated into nothingness. In a moment of terror, she seems truly dead.

I drop to the makeshift bed and take from my backpack the only image I have of my son—an ultrasound from the eighteenth week of pregnancy. In the photo Rory appears in profile, a bright form in dark shadow, with a blurred, busy heart, when the promise of life was still inside him. *Grief fills the room up of my absent child, lies in his bed, walks up and down with me, puts on his pretty looks, repeats his words*...No. Don't do this.

My eye jumps to the desk, to the faded photograph of the infant Celia on her mother's lap. Lost mothers, lost sons; lives delineated by loss. *Maggie + Celia, Oct. '78.*

Suddenly my hair stands on end. I know it before I can form the words. I pull open the desk drawer and take out the *Personal Documents* envelope. Heart pounding, I tear it open, riffling through National Health Service forms, diplomas from Cambridge University and the University of East Anglia, insurance paperwork, vehicle registration, and there it is at the bottom—her birth certificate, dated 23 April 1978. Place of birth: *Portland Hospital for Women and Children.* Name and surname: *Cecelia Jeanne Frost.* Father: *Brian Joseph Frost.*

And there, in official black on white, is her mother's name: *Marguerite Joanne Frost.* Maiden surname: *Alderton.*

Maggie. Short for Marguerite. Marguerite Alderton. The brand-new credit card I found in the bathroom is in the name of Celia's mother, who died in 1981.

Chapter Five

Wednesday
11:46 a.m.

Marguerite Alderton. Celia's mother. Celia must have taken the name to create a new identity for herself. To use after faking a suicide and running away? Hope tightens my throat: *Celia is still alive.* But then why is everything she'd need for her new life—cash, clothes, cell phone, credit card—still at her flat?

I step to the desk and turn on Celia's computer. The grief and fatigue of a few moments ago have disappeared—if Celia is alive, I will find her. While the computer boots up, I search the rest of the desk drawers. I find Celia's checkbook with plenty of blank checks, but all the check registers are empty. Typical of Celia not to keep track of her finances.

Once the computer is up and running, I need a password to access anything—hard drive, e-mail, Internet. Celia lives and works alone—why so much security? I try several combinations of words and numbers that could possibly form Celia passwords, but once I've tried too many, the system locks me out. *Damn.*

On to Plan B. I take a deposit slip from Celia's checkbook and slide it into my pocket. Celia's account is at Barclays, and

Edwina and I passed a Barclays branch about a quarter mile from here, on the way up Hampstead High Street. I grab my jacket and backpack and head out, leaving the door to the flat unlocked behind me. Without a key, I feel I have no choice.

The sky, which earlier featured a muddy sheen like wet concrete, has softened somewhat, to a more inviting shade of powdery gray. Although I never lived in this part of London, the bustling, affluent streets and narrow, cobbled lanes feel familiar. After finishing graduate school at the University of East Anglia in Norwich, Celia and I moved a hundred miles southwest, to London, and shared a tiny basement flat in Clapham, south of the Thames, where we relished our lives as struggling writers. We had virtually no money and survived on small advances from our publishers, along with placing the occasional freelance magazine article. We ate toast with beans or Marmite almost every night, reused tea bags multiple times until nothing but brown water seeped out, and would flip a pound coin to see who got first dibs on our one tubful of fresh bathwater. Now, five years later, I look back on that as the best time of my life, save for the blissful seven and a half months I spent eagerly awaiting the birth of my son.

When Celia and I lived in Clapham, we traveled up to Hampstead twice a month to meet with Rupert Hawes-Dawson, the well-known poet who had been our professor and tutor at the university. Rupert resembled a character from a Merchant-Ivory film: midforties and foppish, impossibly tall, with loose yellow-blond curls tossed across his high forehead and an amiable slouch, as if chronically apologizing for his surprising height. He tended to mumble the end of every sentence and he rolled his own cigarettes with elegant hands that hinted at other, uniquely British, gifts: jam making, sculpture, seduction.

Rupert had offered to tutor us, informally, after graduation, while Celia and I finished our first books. Although Rupert lived in a large London town house with his wife and three children, he kept a modest but well-equipped one-bedroom flat nearby that he used while writing, and that was where we convened for our twice-monthly sessions. While Rupert and Celia discussed Dostoevsky and didactic dualism, I, not privy to their classical education, would sit back and observe their sometimes fiery intellectual discourse.

On the way back to Clapham after our sessions, Celia would be seething, in her contained English way, desperate for a cigarette as she'd smoked all of hers there, and picking apart one of Rupert's off-hand comments about various literary figures. *I mean he said, he actually said, that I overestimated the significance of the thematic continuity that exists between the novels E. M. Forster published before and after his death. Overestimated the significance? Is he serious?*

Walking these same Hampstead streets now, five years later, it is remarkable how memories linger, attached to a place and existing almost in a fourth dimension, immutable and ever-present. The corner newsagent's that today is draped with papers proclaiming TERROR ALERT ON HIGH is where I bought Celia an ice cream and tried to cheer her up after one particularly contentious visit to Rupert in which he dismissed Radclyffe Hall's *The Well of Loneliness*, Celia's favorite novel, as "amateurish and poorly plotted."

Beyond the newsagent's I catch my reflection in the window of a chic French bakery, and it takes me a moment to realize it is me. I am the five-foot-three-inch, dark-haired, pale-skinned woman in a sweater, jeans, jacket, and sneakers. At 145 pounds I still carry an extra fifteen pounds of baby weight; weight from a baby who, had he lived, would not yet weigh fifteen pounds himself. My selfish body clings tightly to the cells that surrounded him, that nurtured him and helped him to grow.

My gaze rises from my own reflection to the watercolor swirl of shapes and forms behind me, floating as if in a dream, a stream of images moving in and out of focus, first sharp, then hazy, then sharp. In the center of the stream, a man. Very clearly a man, with something about him surprisingly precise and specific against the undulating flow of North London street life. He is large and dark, dressed in a black fedora and trench coat. He must be fifteen feet behind me, but aware of him now, I can feel his steady stare slice through my spine. I spin quickly and he is gone, swallowed by the crowd, leaving me to wonder if he was ever really there at all or if he was simply another image from the past, just one of those displaced and lonely ghosts that are said to walk among us.

Shaking myself back to reality I continue on to Barclays, where I have no trouble accessing Celia's personal account information. I simply fill out the deposit slip from Celia's checkbook and hand it to the teller with fifty pounds cash, saying casually, "I'd like to deposit this, and would you mind giving me a printout of my recent transactions? I'm having trouble logging on to my computer at home." I don't even bother employing a fake British accent, assuming the teller is unlikely to know Celia personally.

"Of course, Miss Frost. It will just be a moment." The teller never looks up as she hits a few keys and turns away as a printer whirs busily behind her. The teller returns and hands me a folded piece of paper with Barclays's distinctive logo, a turquoise silhouette of an eagle, at the top. "Here you go," she says with a smile.

I thank her and step away from the window. According to the printout, two days ago, on March 21, Celia withdrew £5,100 from her checking account, leaving a balance of £26, or less than fifty dollars. I have to assume the £5,100 is the money I found stashed behind Celia's mattress. But why? Why take the money in cash? And why, if she faked a suicide and disappeared, is the money still there?

❖

When I get back to Celia's building, the mail has arrived, dumped in a large pile on a ledge just inside the front doorway. Curious, I leaf through the stack of mail and find two envelopes addressed to Celia, hidden among numerous final notices and bills stamped past due. Feeling guilty, I take the mail upstairs and let myself into Celia's flat. For a moment I imagine I will find her inside, waiting for me with a wry grin, narrow hands wrapped around a mug of tea and shoulders hunched as she asks blackly, "You liked my little joke then, did you?"

I drop my backpack on Celia's bed and study the small white envelope that has BB Travel–London/Cardiff as the return address. Inside the envelope is a one-way ferry ticket for Marguerite Alderton, from Holyhead in Wales to Dublin, Ireland, leaving on April 2. I had planned to return home to Chicago a day earlier—April 1. *What the hell?*

I tear open the second, larger envelope, which has no return address. At first I think it's empty, but suddenly something glides out and drifts to the floor. I pick it up and gasp. It's a fuzzy eight-by-ten-inch photograph of Celia standing outside her building, fumbling in her purse as if looking for keys. The photograph appears to have been taken from several yards away with a zoom lens. Across the bottom of the photo someone has scrawled in black marker: *We can make you disappear.*

CHAPTER SIX

Wednesday
12:31 p.m.

Stumbling across the room still clutching the photo and envelope, I sink to the bed as my knees give out beneath me. The woman in the photo is definitely Celia, but it's Celia as I've never seen her: rail thin and haggard, looking ten years too old, with ragged hair bleached brittle-blond and dark shadows beneath her eyes. Celia. What kind of friend allows this to happen? I have been so consumed with my own grief that the rest of the world fell away.

The envelope has no return address, but it was postmarked in London on March 11. Twelve days ago, so it should have arrived last week. Did Celia not know she was in danger? Or had she received other threats, prior to this one?

Instead of calling the police, I phone Celia's therapist, Dr. Fiona Whitaker, whom Celia saw weekly when we lived in Clapham. I never met Dr. Whitaker myself, but I know Celia found her treatment invaluable. Maybe the doctor can tell me if Celia had been receiving threats.

Once I explain what's happened, Dr. Whitaker agrees to see me right away. Before leaving Celia's flat, I stash the ferry ticket, credit card, cell phone, and cash in my backpack and sling it over my shoulder. Better with me than in an unlocked apartment, I decide, especially in light of the threatening photo.

❖

When the Tube to Holland Park stops at Marble Arch, the stuffy, overcrowded carriage empties enough that I think I see, spilling out of an aisle seat at the opposite end of the car, the man I saw earlier, behind me in the bakery window. Even in multicultural central London, his looks are striking. He appears to be a Pacific Islander—Samoan, or perhaps Polynesian. About six foot six and 340 pounds, he has olive skin, a round face, deep-set eyes, and jet-black hair. Dressed in a black trench coat, he balances on his lap a black umbrella, slick with rain.

He looks out the carriage window at a poster for my conference plastered to the rounded station wall, upon which a photograph of my face appears above the words: Keynote Address by Best-Selling Novelist Candee Cronin, Author of *Assignment: Sao Paulo*.

The man glances rapidly from me to the poster and back again. Maybe he's a fan, just trying to figure out if I am Candee Cronin. Maybe.

❖

Dr. Whitaker's office is located on the ground floor of a large semidetached house on a residential street about a quarter mile from the Holland Park Tube. What was once the home's living room has been transformed into a reception area with powder-blue walls, an overstuffed sofa, and fluffy pastel cushions. The receptionist, a cheerful young woman with a Caribbean accent, asks if I'd like coffee or tea, both of which are freshly brewed, and points to a table with paper napkins and a plate of neatly stacked chocolate biscuits. Celia must have hated this place, I realize. Which shows just how desperately she must have felt she needed help.

I take a seat on the sofa and leaf through the glossy pages of *Hello!* magazine, where minor royals are busy marrying their distant (or not-so-distant) cousins, professional soccer players whose names mean nothing to me show off their mansions in Marbella, and an aging '70s rock star cuddles his second Viagra baby. I'm anxious as I wait; the day is passing quickly and there's no sign of Celia. If she is alive, I will find her. *If...*

Dr. Whitaker emerges from her office to greet me and she's younger than I expected. She must have been fresh out of college when Celia first started seeing her. The doctor is pale-skinned and solemn with wire-rim glasses shielding placid green eyes. Her straight, wheat-colored hair is cut plainly, framing her face. "Dr. Fiona Whitaker. A pleasure," she says, extending a small hand from the folds of her long beige sweater.

"Dayle Salvesen," I reply as we shake. "Thank you for seeing me on such short notice."

"Not at all." She motions me into her office and turns to the receptionist. "Lucinda, please hold my calls."

Once inside her office, I take a seat on a small green sofa while she sinks into a big leather chair behind her wooden desk.

"Dr. Whitaker..." I begin.

"Please, call me Fiona," she implores, leaning forward. She slips off her shoes and curls her feet beneath her, cradling a mug of tea.

"Okay, Fiona." I wonder if Celia called her Fiona. Celia would have hated that forced familiarity, dubbing it too American, shorthand for most things she despised.

"Go on," Fiona encourages, raising the mug to her lips and blowing across the surface.

I quickly relate what I know—that the police found Celia's car, with a suicide note inside, early this morning near Waterloo Bridge. They believe Celia jumped to her death, but I found items in Celia's flat that suggest she planned to run away. Then, a threatening message that should have arrived days earlier appeared in today's mail. After summarizing the facts, I ask the doctor what she thinks happened.

"Well, what do *you* think?" she poses, still clasping her mug.

"You mean do I think Celia's still alive?"

"Do you?"

"I'm not sure. You probably remember that Celia and I were once very close..." I stumble, assuming the doctor must have known that, but unsure how much Celia had told her about our relationship. "But we hadn't spoken for several months when she phoned just before Christmas."

"And she rang you then because...?"

"She heard I'd be in London for this conference and she invited me to visit." I have a strange feeling that the doctor knows all this already and is just humoring me.

"Go on," she encourages, sipping her tea.

"I spoke to Celia briefly last week—five, ten minutes to confirm my travel details—and she seemed fine."

"Hmm." The doctor shifts, raising a hip and repositioning her feet.

"Doctor Whitaker—Fiona—in your professional opinion, was Celia suicidal?"

She pauses thoughtfully before replying. "At Celia's last session she seemed positive, upbeat." She pauses again before adding, "She was looking forward to your visit."

"Did she mention receiving any threats?"

"No."

"And nothing in her demeanor made you think she was suicidal?"

"No." She shakes her head. "But suicidal individuals don't always reveal their intentions."

"That's true." I grab a pillow from the sofa and twist it between my fists. "I know Celia attempted suicide twice in the past year, but nothing…"

"I'm sorry—twice?"

"Yes. She slit her wrists last year after her father died. Two months ago she OD'd on sleeping pills."

The doctor looks shocked. "That's not correct. Slashed her wrists, yes, but never overdosed."

"I was told that she had."

"No. I would have known."

My heart lurches. "I can see where Dot Crawford might be mistaken, but Edwina confirmed the story. Celia was taken to the hospital, so it must have been serious."

Fiona appears rattled. Setting down her mug she rises from her chair, grabs an appointment book from atop a rolling cart, and quickly pages through it. "When was this supposed overdose?" she asks, not looking up.

"Two months ago, so…January?" I offer.

Fiona flips several pages back and forth, her pale forehead now deeply furrowed. "I saw Celia twice in December, twice in January, twice last month. She hasn't missed a session, so I would have seen her within two weeks of this supposed overdose. She never said a word."

My mind races. "So either Celia didn't tell you she overdosed, or Dot and Edwina lied."

Fiona taps her bottom lip, then returns to her chair and sits down, craning forward with hands in her lap. "There is another possibility."

"What's that?"

"Maybe she wanted to be *perceived* as suicidal."

"A cry for help?"

She nods. "Possibly."

"But then why not tell you about it too?" I pose. "Wouldn't that have lent credence to the attempt?"

"Perhaps. But if the attempt were not genuine, she might have feared I'd see through the ruse. In that case, better not to tell."

"But that sounds so...deceptive," I argue. "Celia is probably the most honest person I know."

"But we all have secrets, Dayle." She toes the ground softly, spinning slightly in her chair. "Sometimes even from ourselves."

We speak for another twenty minutes, but I'm frustrated that the doctor can't, or won't, provide much insight into Celia's mental status or recent state of mind. Realizing that I can probably find out more on my own, I thank Dr. Whitaker for her time. As I rise from the green sofa, she motions for me to stay seated.

"Before you go, there is something else." She winces as if she's said too much.

"What is it?"

"It might not mean anything, but until we know for certain..." She fiddles with a ballpoint pen, scribbling circles on a notepad.

"What?"

"Very well." She rises from her chair and steps across the room to a tall metal cupboard, then withdraws a key from her sweater pocket and unlocks the cupboard door. Standing on tiptoe she reaches to the top shelf and pulls down a stuffed manila folder, sealed with tape. I rise from the sofa and walk toward her.

"I'm not certain I should give you this." She holds the folder tightly to her chest and crosses her arms, almost daring me to take it.

"What is it?"

"Celia's manuscript," she says, just above a whisper.

"What kind of manuscript?"

She shakes her head. "I don't know. I didn't open it. Celia asked me to store it here."

"Was that unusual?"

"Not at all. I gather that her flat is rather a shambles and she felt it best to keep a backup copy somewhere off-site."

"When did she give this to you?"

She purses her lips, deep in thought. "About a month ago? Late February."

Dr. Whitaker hands me the folder and I am silent, allowing its weight to register in my wrists as I absorb its special resonance, its embryonic heft. For a writer, a manuscript is a sacred object, an article of faith, not to be touched by another without permission. As close as Celia and I once were, I know, instinctively, that I should never put my hand on her book without asking her first.

"And you have no idea what's inside?" I softly stroke the folder with my fingertips, wondering when Celia herself last touched this surface.

"I'm sorry, no." Dr. Whitaker looks away sadly, shaking her head. "I wish now that I had questioned her, probed a bit deeper as to what she was feeling. But as I mentioned, she seemed fine at the time. Busy, optimistic, upbeat. Things were going well. I saw no reason to be concerned."

"Can I take this with me?"

"Please do." She nods vigorously. "Perhaps it contains some clue as to what's happened to Celia." She pauses, raising her narrow shoulders. "At least one can hope."

❖

I return to the Holland Park Tube, and while waiting for the train I take the folder from my backpack and peel open the seal. Inside is a document of about 350 unbound pages of A4 paper, single-sided and double-spaced, printed in a 12-point Courier font. I see only text, no graphics or photos, and nothing inserted between the pages. This appears, at first glance, anyway, to be nothing more than an ordinary manuscript.

When the train arrives I climb aboard, grab a seat, and begin reading:

AMONG THE UNCONSOLED
A Novel
by Cecelia Frost

She lifted her hand, she knocked on the door, and then she died. Her last actions were just that simple—battering her frostbitten fingers against the half-inch-thick plate of glass, leaving her last breath ghosted onto the shiny surface like an icy museum piece, where it would remain undisturbed until spring.

It was the middle of the night and I might have mistaken the knocking for the sound of the windows rattling in the wind, the bitter wind that sweeps in from the North Sea, unbidden and unimpeded, and weaves itself into dreams...

I recognize the text, albeit not the title. This is Celia's first novel, never published, that she worked on in graduate school. At that time it had been called *The Harmony Argument* and it concerned a young musician whose personal life fell apart just as her career took off. Rupert Hawes-Dawson had been particularly critical of the novel-in-progress, both inside class and out, and eventually Celia put the project aside to focus on writing short stories, ultimately collected and published to great acclaim in *West of Blessing, North of Hope*.

Scanning the manuscript, I remember enough of the earlier draft, even after several years, to realize that this is a substantially not just different, but improved version of the text. Did Celia rewrite the novel in hopes of finally getting it published? I didn't think she had written any fiction since her second book and first novel, *The Pursuit of Sorrow*, was a critical and commercial failure three years ago.

Was there something within the text of this revised manuscript, a note or a clue, that Celia hoped we'd find in the event that something happened to her? *Come on, Celia. I'm here for you. Let me help you. Tell me what I need to know.*

❖

I leave the Central Line at Tottenham Court Road and wait on the Northern Line platform for the next train back to Hampstead. Still absorbed in Celia's novel, I am reminded of what a gifted writer she is, of the pristine beauty of her sentences and her ability to convey, in just a few words, depths of despair and utter desolation.

As I read I am only vaguely aware that the train is taking a long time to arrive. I can feel the weight of bodies gathering behind me as people mass on the narrow concrete platform.

A hot, anxious, impatient press of flesh inches me forward as I instinctively search for open space in this dense and humid tunnel, which seems to grow smaller by the second. The layering of body upon body thins the air to a dank and sour cloud of carbon dioxide.

I feel the train before I see it, feel it as a rising rumble beneath my feet from somewhere down the line. Then I catch a slim glimpse of light in the tunnel, on the edge of my peripheral vision. The waiting crowd stiffens, straightening in expectation and pressing me toward the warning painted on the floor in white: MIND THE GAP.

Suddenly something strikes me from the side, knocking the air from my lungs as the rumble of the train picks up speed. My hands shoot out to steady myself and Celia's manuscript flies from my arms, slips of white paper rising like doves, darting, dispersing, and fluttering back to earth. I reach out to grab the pages before they are whisked away on the rushing tunnel wind and I lose my footing, tumbling to the platform. My cheek strikes concrete and pain echoes through my skull. A woman screams; voices shout for help. Stunned, I cannot move my arms or legs. Hands reach down to grab me; someone pulls my jacket but the fabric slips.

A disk of intense yellow light appears in the tunnel, expanding quickly until it explodes into a white-hot corona. I close my eyes, too frightened to weep, too scared to pray beyond asking God to take me quickly.

Rising above the metallic shriek of wheels on steel comes a jagged, jarring wail, a noise I will remember forever and which I was told I could not have heard: the high-pitched rushing cry of my child entering the world—the only sound he uttered in the fifty-three minutes that he lived.

CHAPTER SEVEN

Wednesday
2:21 p.m.

I am not even certain that I'm still alive until I feel the damp, cold concrete of the station floor rising into my spine, followed by the thrust of foreign hands tapping my cheeks and poking my throat. I blink rapidly and open my eyes to find two women crouched over me, one on either side. They must be mother and daughter; the younger, about thirty, is a slim, freckled, long-haired brunette with high cheekbones and a pointy chin; the elder woman, midfifties, has the same pert, pretty features, but on her they have been expanded, loosened, and softly lined.

"Are you all right, love?" the mother asks anxiously, stroking my hand.

"I...I think so," I reply as blood rushes into my limbs. "What happened? Did I fall onto the tracks?"

"No, nothing half that dramatic. Just tripped on the platform." Dark pupils dance within the daughter's bright green eyes. "But you looked a right mess!"

I blink and look around, trying to clear my head. So that explains why the platform, formerly packed with people, is now nearly empty and why the women's voices echo dully against the damp brick walls. The train must have arrived, released its passengers, and swallowed up new ones, all while I was in la-la land.

"How long was I out of it?" Fingers still shaking, I explore my jaw and cheek, mining for injuries.

The mother glances at her watch and frowns. "Can't be five minutes? Three, maybe four."

I sit up and clutch my head, waiting for the world to stop spinning. "Help me up," I ask.

"Are you well enough?" the daughter poses breathlessly.

"Only one way to find out."

The women lift me to my feet, each taking a shoulder. Once I'm fully upright and my head clears, I look down and see what remains of Celia's manuscript: an uneven stack of papers spread limply on top of my backpack, which is balanced near the platform's edge in a deflated heap. As I turn I see dozens of pages scattered up and down the tracks, some intact, others confettied into tiny shreds.

Frantic, I grab as many loose pages as I can and stuff them into the backpack, which still contains the cell phone, credit card, and £5000 cash. "Please help me," I ask the women. "We've got to get these papers before the next train arrives." An Edgware train is due in three minutes, according to the electronic sign blinking steadily above my head.

Dutifully the women comply, collecting handfuls of torn, stained, and crumpled pages and passing them to me. We've got most of the papers off the platform when a rumble deep beneath our feet heralds the next train. For one desperate moment I look down at the papers still littering the tracks.

"Come away from there, dear," the mother beckons gently, taking my arm. "You can't salvage that lot."

"But you don't understand," I protest as the daughter slips the backpack, containing the remnants of Celia's novel, over my shoulder. "This manuscript wasn't even mine."

They raise their palms and shrug sadly, indicating that my cause is lost. Meanwhile, a dozen or so passengers who have traveled down the escalator gather on the platform in twos and threes.

"Can you manage?" The mother lifts her chin toward the approaching train. I nod. My ears ring, my body shivers, but I know if I don't get on the next train, right now, I will never again ride a subway in my life. I close my eyes as blood rockets through my skull. The brick walls constrict and the train becomes a bullet in a barrel, a malevolently vicious thing. The mother-daughter duo steps closer and absorbs me into the closed circle of their interior, where I revel in the foreign warmth.

The train arrives and shudders to a stop, inches from my face. A buzzer sounds, the doors steam open, and for a moment I am paralyzed. Then I surrender to the force of anxious bodies propelling me into the carriage, where I collapse into the first seat beside the door. The train lurches forward, pauses, then picks up speed. *I did it. I survived.*

From Tottenham Court Road there are seven stops to Belsize Park, the station closest to Celia's flat. *Goodge Street, Warren Street, Euston*—the stations blink by through the windows, offering brief respites of warmth and light between blinding stretches of damp and rapid darkness. My body relaxes, carving out a space for the pain in my left wrist, a pain that increases with each passing minute. By Mornington Crescent I've lost the dent between wrist and hand; by Camden Town, purple and black bruises breach my forearm. By Chalk

Farm, my fingers have stiffened and I can no longer make a fist.

When I emerge from the station at Belsize Park I am briefly surprised by the hazy daylight filtering through a lacy veil of clouds. It's less than an hour since I left Dr. Whitaker, but the intense darkness of the Underground seems to have lasted forever, consuming the brightness of several days.

Instead of returning to Celia's flat, I walk the short distance from the Tube station to the Royal Free Hospital, a multilevel, modern-looking structure with a large illuminated canopy over the main street-level entrance. I'll lose precious time waiting for an X-ray, but what else can I do? My wrist is beyond painful now, and as swollen and shiny as bruised fruit.

Fluorescent yellow ambulances dart in and out of the lower-level loading bay, near where I enter A&E—the accident and emergency department—through the sliding glass doors. I give my details at the reception desk and am assessed by a triage nurse in a prim, old-fashioned uniform of robin's egg blue. She declares me green–Priority 4, meaning my injury is not life threatening. This also means I will probably be waiting here forever, until all the more serious cases have been seen to.

As I take my seat in the hot, crowded, antiseptic-smelling waiting room across from a man in a soiled boilersuit pressing a bloodied rag to his forehead, I try not to think about the last time I was inside a hospital, five months ago. Instead I attempt to keep my wrist elevated, as the triage nurse instructed, above my heart. This being England, there is no ice.

A large, flat-screen TV anchored to the wall scrolls rapid, capital-letter updates about the ongoing terror alert, but the ill and injured assembled beneath it seem strangely blasé. I turn away and take out my cell phone. Edwina's lecture probably finished at two or two thirty. It's nearly three o'clock now and she answers on the second ring.

"Edwina, it's Dayle."

"Dayle—any news?" She sounds frantic.

"Not exactly." I fill her in on the threatening photo and Dr. Whitaker not knowing of Celia's overdose. Then I tell her about my accident.

She gasps. "Were you pushed?"

"I don't know. It was crowded. I wasn't paying attention..." My voice catches. "I lost most of Celia's manuscript when I fell."

"Sit tight. I'll be right there."

"You don't have to—"

"I insist." She pauses. "As would Celia."

After hanging up with Edwina, I phone DC Callaway. My first question is whether there's been any news about Celia. She says that there hasn't.

"You should probably know, I had an accident at Tottenham Court Road Tube this afternoon. I fell—or was pushed—to the platform," I explain.

"Well, which was it?"

"I'm sorry?"

"Did you fall or were you pushed?"

"I'm not sure—"

"Did you report the incident?"

"No. I was too shaken up."

She exhales heavily. "You should file an incident report at the station."

"But I want to report it to the police. In case..."

"In case what?"

"In case there's some connection to Celia."

"Should there be?"

"No. I don't know." I pause, rubbing my eyes. "Look, I'm waiting for an X-ray. Your station is on Rosslyn Hill, right? That's close by. I'll come over when I'm done—"

"No," she interrupts with an irritated sigh. "Don't bother. If you feel the pressing need to make a statement, I'll meet you there. The Royal Free? I'll be there shortly."

"Oh." I'm not sure what else to say. "Well, thanks, then," I add, but she has already hung up.

❖

I am called into an exam room more quickly than I expected and after an initial and rather brusque examination of my forearm, wrist, hand, and fingers, the doctor orders an X-ray. While the technician positions my aching arm, the pain worsens and I feel sick. Waves of nausea lash the sides of my stomach while my throat tightens and dries. Something about the room—the heat, the lights, the smell—brings back too many terrible memories. The technician, a full-figured black woman with kind, round eyes, senses my anxiety and tries to comfort me, but that only makes it worse; her detached compassion, so clinically efficient, bruises my nerves and reopens old wounds.

I close my eyes and hold my breath. As the X-ray clicks, I feel an invisible stream of energy moving through me. In a moment of clarity, the entire hospital comes into focus and I can sense everything happening within this building, from the suffocating sorrow of the soon-to-be-bereaved to the desolation of the newly dead, who release their heat alone, untended and unconsoled. I have to get out of here. Now.

When the doctor returns to the exam room he holds a film up to the light and says I have a sprained wrist and a hairline fracture of the fifth metacarpal, the bone that runs between the wrist and the little finger. He shows me the ghostly bone on the X-ray and helpfully traces the line of the fracture with a capped pen. It looks fine to me, but what do I know? When I look at the X-ray, I am primarily surprised that anything inside of me is so small.

I ask for a fiberglass cast but I'm told that, given the position of the break, the cast must be plaster. The cast is set and the plaster still drying when I hear from the hallway the insistent tap-tap-tap of Edwina's Docs coming closer. "Edwina? In here," I call out. A moment later she pulls open the striped curtain and her square shoulders block the light. Her gray eyes widen as she notices the still-damp cast.

"Oh no—it must be broken." She strides toward me and slips her arm around my neck, carefully avoiding my left side as she pats my back in stiff circles. Edwina smells of strong soap and sandalwood and the coarse coils of her closely cropped hair graze my cheek as she pulls back, placing her hand firmly atop my shoulder.

"Hairline fracture," I explain, nodding toward my immobilized arm. "Tiny, apparently, but broken."

"No worries. Bones heal." She flashes that gap-toothed grin. "It's not your heart."

I look down again at my forearm, now encased in pristine white plaster of paris, with my bruised and swollen fingers poking out at the end like half-wrapped sausages. "I lost most of Celia's manuscript," I whisper. "Celia gave it to Dr. Whitaker for safekeeping." I try not to cry around British people but my eyes burn and tears clog my throat.

"Never mind. Celia must have another copy. In her flat, perhaps. Or on her computer." Edwina motions for me to lie back on the exam table as she straightens the paper pillow behind my head and smooths my hair. Fussing over me, she seems more feminine: still a solid presence, but her soft gray eyes are warmer, crinkling when she smiles, and lines of kindness surround her generous mouth. I realize with a stab of envy how lucky Celia was to have been intimate with this stunning woman.

"Are you going to be all right?" Edwina frowns.

"What do you mean?"

"You're quite pale. And trembling." She squeezes the fingers on my good hand. "Perhaps you should stay here and let the doctors look after you until you're feeling better."

"No, I'll be fine. I've got to get out of here and figure out what happened to Celia. I've already wasted too much time."

"What have you learned so far?" She motions for me to slide over, then she sits on the table beside me with her hand cupping my knee.

"I'm convinced Celia planned to leave London," I explain. "I think something went wrong with her plan, but I believe she is still alive."

Edwina looks down and shakes her head sadly. "I'm certain she's dead."

Her comment startles me. "Why do you say that?"

"She still loved me, even after the breakup. She wouldn't have left without saying good-bye. Unless..." Her voice trails away.

"Unless?" I ask softly.

"Unless she had decided to die. And knew I'd try to stop her."

Before I can respond, a blue-uniformed nurse bustles back into the room, breaking the somber mood. After checking that my cast is dry, she tells me I can leave. "The hand should be X-rayed again in four weeks—the cast can come off in six," she explains. "You may need to take some paracetamol for the pain."

"Let's get out of here." Edwina forces a smile as the nurse leaves. "Hospitals are dreadful places."

"We can't," I reply. "DC Callaway is coming to take my statement."

She shrugs. "Well let's wait outside then and catch her on the way in."

After settling my bill with the payment department, Edwina and I walk back toward the elevator and pass a young dark-haired girl, head down, walking in the other direction. Edwina stops suddenly, pivots, and calls out, "Tatiana?"

The girl stops and looks over her shoulder, her whole body quivering. Edwina beckons me to follow as she approaches the girl. "Tatiana?" she asks again. "It's Edwina. Celia's friend."

The girl nods slowly, looking terrified.

"Why are you here?"

Tatiana stares blankly. Although the size of a ten- or eleven-year-old, her face looks much older with creased eyelids, sallow cheeks, and greasy hair separated into thin strands. She is dressed shabbily in a floor-length denim skirt and a beige hooded sweatshirt, half-zipped, revealing a stained white T-shirt beneath.

"Where is Sophie?" Edwina asks.

An expression of relief flits across the girl's hollow features. "Come," she says with a nod, clasping Edwina's hand and guiding us down the corridor.

At the end we turn to the left, and a short distance later Tatiana stops at the entrance to a small waiting room with muted lights, pastel carpet, and a burbling fish tank. The only person inside the room is a thin blond woman, midthirties, sitting on a dark sofa, shoulders hunched as she stares at a tissue stretched taut between her fists.

"Excuse me—Sophie?" Edwina asks softly as we enter the room.

Instantly the woman's head shoots up and she squints, trying to focus. "Edwina?"

"Yes. Sophie, this is Dayle Salvesen, Celia's friend from the States. Dayle, Sophie Jameson. Sophie is the director at Hope House, a charity for homeless women and girls."

As we shake, Sophie's hand is cold and clammy. "Nice to meet you," I say.

"Likewise," she replies, clearing her throat.

"We passed Tatiana in the corridor," Edwina says gently. "Sophie, what's wrong? Why are you here?"

Sophie pauses, glances uncertainly at Tatiana, then speaks. "It's Mileva. Celia may have mentioned her. A trafficked sex worker from Ukraine. Someone botched her backstreet abortion two weeks ago and now the surgeons are trying to save her uterus." Sophie exhales heavily. "She's fourteen years old."

"I'm so sorry." Looking uncomfortable, Edwina takes a seat beside Sophie and glances up at me.

I nod.

"Sophie, I have news that might be upsetting," Edwina begins. "Celia's gone missing and may have killed herself."

"My God." Sophie looks up with a start. "What happened?"

"We're not certain. Her car was discovered this morning near Waterloo Bridge with a suicide note, but there's been no sign of Celia."

"Well she can't have killed herself," Sophie replies with surprising vigor.

"How can you be sure?" I jump in.

"She had arranged to meet us tonight at Hope House. Drop off a large package, she said."

"Package?" Edwina and I ask in unison.

"Yes." Sophie draws a breath.

"What kind of package?"

She shrugs. "I'm not certain. But from the way she spoke, I expect she meant money."

CHAPTER EIGHT

Wednesday
4:35 p.m.

"What made you think she was delivering money?" As I step closer, my shadow crosses Sophie's face and Tatiana scurries to Sophie's side, guarding her from beside the sofa.

Sophie frowns. "I'm not certain. Celia was hesitant to say too much."

"Did she often deliver money?"

Sophie stiffens. "Occasionally."

My mind flashes to the modesty of Celia's flat and the stacks of overdue bills. "Where did the money come from?"

Sophie shakes her head. "No idea."

"Weren't you curious?"

"Not particularly."

My frustration grows. "Why not?"

Sophie scowls. "I run a shelter for vulnerable young women, Miss Salvesen. We survive through charity donations. Forgive me if I don't feel the need to explore the origin of every penny we receive."

"How much money have you gotten from Celia?"

"I don't know."

"A rough estimate, then?"

"I really couldn't say."

My arm throbs and I press it to my side, trying to deaden the pain. "Just in the last few months?"

Sophie sniffs and dabs her nose with the tissue. "I'd have to check the books."

"Sophie, if you know something, anything, please tell us," Edwina pleads, rising from the sofa to stand at my side. "For Celia's sake."

Sophie sighs, reaching for another tissue. "I'm afraid I can't help you."

I am about to press Sophie for more information when a young nurse enters the room and approaches us, clearing her throat. "Miss Jameson? The surgeon would like to speak with you."

Edwina touches my back and gestures toward the doorway. "We'd best leave," she says softly. "Sophie and Tatiana will want to be there when Mileva wakes up."

"All right," I reluctantly reply. Sophie hands me her business card and asks me to phone her when I have any news. Then Edwina and I say good-bye to Sophie and Tatiana and make our way down the corridor. Edwina and I are at the elevator before either of us speaks.

"Do you think Celia intended to give Sophie the money from behind her bed?" Edwina proposes.

"What do you mean?"

"Could that have been the delivery she planned to make tonight?"

The elevator arrives. We step inside and the lights flicker as the door rattles closed. Edwina pushes the button for the lower ground floor.

"Possibly," I reply. "But then Celia would have had no money for her new life."

"Unless…"

"Unless what?"

"Unless she wasn't planning a new life. Maybe she planned to give Sophie the money and *then* kill herself."

"I doubt it." My voice sounds hollow and metallic in the closed cavern of the elevator car. "Why get the credit card, the cell phone, the Dublin maps? Celia was planning escape, not suicide."

"I want to believe that, I really do. But—"

"But what?" We reach the lower ground floor and the doors slide open. We emerge into a cold and sterile corridor that is bathed in a sickly greenish light.

"You didn't see Celia at her worst." Edwina turns to face me, eyes flashing. "When her father died, when she cut her wrists, when she overdosed. Celia has a darkness inside her, a gaping wound, a grief that never goes away. She keeps it at bay with her sarcasm, her passion for her work, even her love-hate relationship with writing. Therapy and medication help. But even with plenty of support, if she felt overwhelmed, despairing…it scares me, knowing what she's capable of."

Celia was once my lover—how could I not have known everything about her? But as Edwina speaks I don't picture Celia of the threatening photograph from this afternoon, the haggard, bone-thin, sallow bleach blonde; no, I see Celia at age thirteen, then only four feet eleven inches tall, with hair dyed black and a black leather Harley jacket, standing onstage at Fillmore Junior High School in Green Bay, demanding to audition for the part of Jesus in the school production of *Godspell*, even though her voice was only average and she hated wearing makeup. To Celia, it was worth it. Anything to strike a blow for local feminism while simultaneously outraging the Fillmore PTA.

"You're right," I admit to Edwina. "You're much closer to Celia now than I am."

"Dayle, this isn't a competition." Edwina folds her long arms and leans back against the wall opposite the elevator, looking defeated. "I just want to know what's happened to her."

"I know. So do I."

As we return to the A&E reception area, I glimpse DC Callaway shuttling through the sliding glass doors. Only five hours have elapsed since I last saw the detective, but the advancing day seems to have aged her, adding years to her appearance. Her oily beige trench coat flaps in the breeze and her thin, wispy hair, which earlier offered only the slightest hint of a style, has collapsed flatly against her forehead. Even from this distance she smells of a hastily smoked cigarette, obliterated by an angry heel and still smoldering on the steps outside the hospital entrance.

After introducing Edwina and exchanging brief greetings, I suggest we sit down and perhaps get something to eat. There's a chic-looking restaurant on this floor of the hospital, along with a smaller café, but DC Callaway doesn't have time, even for a meager cup of tea, she informs us. So instead we find a few chairs on the perimeter of the A&E reception area, beside a bank of vending machines, and talk there.

I begin by telling Callaway about my accident at the Tube station. As she takes notes, her nicotine-stained fingers press her pencil stub so tightly that her yellow nail beds turn white. A troubled V appears between her eyebrows and frown lines tug her firmly set mouth. "Hmm," she offers. "Go on." "Yes?" "Uh-huh." She seems concerned mostly with whether

I saw whoever pushed me, if indeed anyone did. "A man or a woman?" she asks.

"I don't know. I never turned to look," I explain. "I felt something, lost my footing, then hit the ground."

She pivots, coughing into her clenched fist. "Well, you must have some sense of the person. Large? Small?"

"I really don't know."

A somber-looking Southeast Asian boy of about eleven with large dark eyes approaches the vending machine, coins pinched between his fingertips. Edwina nods him forward, indicating he may use the machine.

"And you didn't see height, hair color, clothing?" Callaway presses.

I shake my head. "No. Nothing. I was reading Celia's manuscript, so I wasn't paying much attention."

A can of Coke rattles through the vending machine chute as Callaway draws in her thin bottom lip and squints at her notes. "Is there anything else you can tell me that might be helpful? Anything you heard? A noise? Anything?"

"Not at Tottenham Court Road," I say slowly, watching the boy walk away with his drink in hand, "but earlier in the day a man seemed to be following me. I wonder now if there's some connection between that man and my accident."

"Followed you?" Callaway's voice sounds practiced and casual, but her pupils briefly flare.

"I think so. I can't be sure." I describe the man I saw on the way to Celia's bank and then later on the Tube. While I speak, Edwina taps my shoulder and reminds me to keep my broken hand elevated, as the doctor advised.

After I finish my description of the man, Callaway promises she'll look into reports of any other recent assaults on the Tube or in and around the stations. "But I must admit, this sounds like nothing more than an unfortunate accident," she warns. After reviewing her notes, she says I'm free to leave. I am secretly relieved—my wrist aches and I just want to rest for a while before the conference.

"There is something else," I add as we rise from the narrow plastic chairs.

"Oh?" Callaway jams an arm into her trench coat and wrestles it over her shoulder. "What's that?"

I glance at Edwina, who nods for me to continue.

"When Celia's mail arrived this afternoon, there was an envelope containing a photo of her standing outside her flat. Someone had scribbled on the bottom, *We can make you disappear*."

Callaway scowls as she hikes her canvas messenger bag over her shoulder and centers it beneath her arm. "Where and when was the envelope postmarked?"

"London. Twelve days ago."

Her sparse eyebrows rise. "Twelve days ago? And it arrived today?"

"Yes. Maybe Celia didn't even realize she was in danger."

"Perhaps not." Callaway looks away uneasily.

"What is it?" I ask.

Sudden color flushes her ashy cheeks. "Nothing."

"You looked as if you were about to say something," I probe.

"No."

"What is it?" Edwina insists.

Callaway draws a deep breath and then exhales forcefully, shoulders plunging. "You should probably know."

"Know what?" My mind races.

"Information might emerge from this case that will shock or disturb you."

"What kind of information?" I ask.

Callaway's hazel eyes dart furtively from me to Edwina and back again. "Cecelia Frost may not have been as saintly as she appeared."

"What are you implying?" Edwina steps in front of Callaway and folds her arms across her chest, rising to her full, imposing height.

"We have uncovered evidence that Celia engaged with the criminal element," Callaway explains. "The Russian Mafia, to be precise—ringleaders of the international sex trade."

"Of course she engaged with them." Edwina moves to within inches of Callaway's face. "That was how she got women and girls who'd been trafficked into Britain off the streets. But Celia always acted legally."

"Well, she does have a criminal record," Callaway offers, standing her ground.

"Only very minor offenses," Edwina counters quickly.

"Wait a minute—Celia has a criminal record?" This is news to me.

"Oh, didn't you know?" Callaway's glance at me over Edwina's shoulder contains a smirk of superiority.

"No, I didn't," I admit.

"Oh yes. As I recall, she was charged with aggravated trespass, breaking and entering, criminal damage, and breach of the peace." Callaway lists the charges as a succession of sharpened daggers. "And they may only be minor offenses, as you say, Miss Adebayo," Callaway pauses dramatically, "but taken as a whole they paint a rather compelling portrait of someone who plays fast and loose with the law."

"You're not being fair, DC Callaway," Edwina argues. "Celia may have faced serious charges, but the convictions were on counts far less serious, which you know as well as I."

I cannot believe what I am hearing. "Wait a minute—let's backtrack a bit here. DC Callaway, are you suggesting that Celia's disappearance is related to her work at the relief center?"

Callaway sighs. "I'm afraid that's a possibility."

"Yes, but what evidence do you have?" Edwina's voice deepens with alarm. "Other than innuendo and character assassination?"

"I'm sorry. I may have already said too much. This is still an open investigation." Callaway steps back and pats her coat pockets in a furtive search for cigarettes. "I will let you know as soon as there's any news."

We say our good-byes and leave through the sliding glass doors. Edwina and I watch from the ambulance bay as DC Callaway gets into her car, slams the door, and lights a cigarette before driving away. "Charming woman," Edwina mutters.

I smile in spite of myself. "Who knew there were so many shades of beige?" Edwina links my good arm with hers and together we traverse the parking lot. The skies have cleared since earlier this afternoon and a clean scent of cold, rain-washed concrete fills the streets as we begin the short walk back to Celia's flat. The early evening is brisk, even pleasant, but my mood remains dark.

"So Celia has a criminal record?" I ask gently.

Edwina stiffens beside me. "Yes, but only minor offenses," she says defensively.

"The things Callaway mentioned don't sound minor." I pause, choosing my words carefully. "Especially when taken as a whole."

"Come now, Dayle, don't be so naïve."

"How am I being naïve?"

"Celia engaged in work that is risky and challenging. She deals with some very bad people, but only for a greater good. It's not as if she sits in an ivory tower writing all day."

Ignoring the insult, I continue. "I understand that her work is difficult but—"

"Most of the charges Callaway listed—charges that were dropped, by the way—came after Celia helped organize some of the protests in London last year after the government introduced a huge rise in university tuition fees. Celia was brave enough to stand up for her beliefs and now this, this *detective constable*, wants to paint Celia as some common criminal. I'm sorry, I am just not having it."

"It's okay," I reassure her. "I wasn't questioning Celia's character. I know the kind of person she is. I was simply trying to understand Callaway's accusations, put them into some sort of context."

Edwina softens slightly, squeezing my uninjured arm. "Sorry, Dayle." The gap-toothed grin briefly reappears. "I didn't mean to attack you. I'm just rather protective of my lovely girl, that's all. Protective and proud."

"No problem. I understand."

But as we approach Celia's building, I'm still troubled. There is apparently so much I don't know about Celia. Suicide attempts. A criminal record. What *else* don't I know?

We enter the run-down mansion at 10 Rosslyn Hill and ascend the rickety staircase to the second floor, stopping in front of flat number 5. Edwina taps the unlocked door, which swings open at her touch. She steps inside and gasps.

I duck under her arm and enter the flat, which has been thoroughly ransacked. Clothes are strewn everywhere, drawers pulled from the dresser and overturned, loose papers cascading across the desk. The cupboards have been hastily thrown open; dry goods and dishware, swept from the shelves, lay torn and broken on the floor.

"My God," I whisper, turning a full circle and trying to comprehend the scene. Edwina recovers before I do and quickly inventories Celia's few valuables: computer and office equipment, case files, some family jewelry.

"Nothing significant seems to be missing," she pronounces. "In fact, I can't see that anything is missing at all."

"The money," I say suddenly.

"What money?"

"Whoever was here must have wanted the five thousand pounds from behind Celia's mattress."

Edwina lunges toward the bed.

"It isn't there."

She stops suddenly.

"It's still in my backpack," I explain.

She looks at me, wide-eyed.

"It's been there, along with the cell phone and credit card, since early this afternoon."

CHAPTER NINE

Wednesday
5:08 p.m.

"You mean to say you've been walking around London with five thousand pounds in your rucksack?"

I nod. "After receiving the threatening photo, I figured the money was safer with me than in an unlocked apartment," I explain. "And by the looks of this place, I was right."

"What are we going to do?" Edwina collapses into a kitchen chair and covers her face.

"Call DC Callaway, I guess, then get ready for my speech."

Edwina looks up in shock. "You still intend to go?"

"I have to. I'm the keynote speaker."

She shakes her head. "Dayle, you've had no sleep for what, two days? You arrive to find your friend may be dead, you get pushed onto a train platform and break your arm, and now the flat where you're meant to spend the night is ransacked. I think the organizers would understand if you canceled."

"I can't," I argue. "I made a commitment. And the conference might help take my mind off things. At least for a while."

I pick up the phone and dial Callaway's numbers, office and mobile, but both go to voice mail, where I leave what I hope are not-too-frantic messages, telling her the flat's been ransacked and asking her to return my call.

Edwina and I exchange looks. "Now what?" she asks.

"Clean up the place. Then I better get dressed." While Edwina sweeps up the broken dishware and tidies the kitchenette, I collect the scattered papers and pile them on Celia's desk, then fold Celia's clothing and bundle the items back into her wardrobe and dresser. Once the flat is at least navigable again, I use my good arm to clear a spot on top of Celia's mattresses. With Edwina's help I lift my suitcase to the bed and open it, surveying the contents. "This is strange," I say.

"What's that?" She peers over my shoulder and into the case.

"Whoever ransacked the flat had time to rummage through drawers and papers, overturn lamps, do some major damage, and yet, this suitcase wasn't touched."

She frowns. "So?"

"This is Louis Vuitton luggage. Inside there's a ruby pendant, a Rolex watch, a ruby-and-diamond ring, and two cashmere sweaters. We assume whoever was here wanted the cash from behind Celia's bed, but they could have taken this suitcase and sold it, along with everything inside, for much more than that. And there's a MacBook in my laptop bag that hasn't been touched."

"Maybe they wanted that cash for a reason," Edwina offers.

"Like what?"

She shrugs. "Because they wouldn't have time to sell your things? Or maybe there's something special about that money—the serial numbers, perhaps."

I slump to the bed beside the suitcase, which slides against my thigh. "I give up. This is just so bizarre."

I glance from the clock, which shows quarter after five, to my broken hand. "I'd love to wash my hair before the conference."

"I can help."

"Really? That would be great." I secretly hoped she'd volunteer but wasn't sure how to ask.

"Certainly. First, just allow me to tidy the bathroom. Celia is not exactly house-proud, as you can see." Edwina pulls off her Doc Martens and rolls up the sleeves of her powder-blue Oxford shirt, revealing solid, muscular arms, a shade of mahogany one degree darker than the skin of her face and neck. Somehow she finds, within the ruined kitchen, hidden beneath the sink, a bottle of dish soap, a short-handled scrub brush, and a box of bicarbonate of soda.

I take off my sweater and observe at the bathroom door, barefoot, in only a bra and jeans. She works quickly, scrubbing the mold and soap scum from the corners of the tub, then salting the surfaces with the bicarbonate and rinsing the whole thing clean. She is thoughtful and focused as she works, probably not even aware of the melodic tune she hums beneath her breath.

With a damp cloth she wipes the sink, the edges of the tub, and the top of the toilet before folding a large bath towel and placing it on the floor. She beckons me into the bathroom and motions for me to kneel, bracing my elbows on the side of the tub. I curl the cast to my chest, where the sudden brush of pebbled plaster gives me chills. "Cover the cast with your opposite hand," Edwina advises, stationed behind me. "So it doesn't get wet." My swollen fingers barely bend as I tuck them beneath my chin.

"Can you get closer?" Edwina gently presses my spine and I feel the weight of her shadow over my shoulder.

"I think so." I scoot forward until my knees touch the tub. Then I lift my neck and bow my head, bobbing and craning to the height of her outstretched palm.

"Yes. Just like that," she encourages as she turns on the hot and cold taps, letting the water mingle as it flows through the plastic attachment that serves as a makeshift showerhead. An intermittent hiss of water droplets flashes across her hand as she checks the temperature, waiting patiently for it to rise.

"This always takes forever," she whispers, half exasperated.

"That's all right." I press closer and breathe in the warm steam billowing from the bottom of the tub, which now smells clean and briny, retaining only the faintest memory of mold.

She says something, but I can't make out her words above the water's murmur, churning so close to my ear. "I'm sorry?"

"Shampoo—honeysuckle rose?"

"Fine," I reply.

I close my eyes and surrender to Edwina's touch. Her strong hands are firm and confident as she lathers the shampoo and scrubs my scalp, massaging with her fingertips. She moves in smooth circles that start at my crown and move outward, skirting the edges of my temples and brushing the notch atop my spine. She hums as she works, in time with the rhythm of the water.

After rinsing the shampoo she applies conditioner, which smells like chamomile and gardenia, earthier and more pungent than the shampoo. The scent, condensed and enlivened by the steam, circles my head like a perfumed garland. My consciousness flickers, winnowing to a pinpoint, and I wish I could kneel here forever, blessed by her expert hands and the warmth of the water.

Edwina rinses away the conditioner, carefully clearing the folds behind my earlobes. She turns off the taps, and as the last droplets sputter through the showerhead now coiled at the bottom of the tub, she wraps a clean towel around my head and pats my hairline dry.

A gentle tap on my back informs me I may stand. I rise unsteadily, balancing the awkward weight of my plaster-cast wrist. Edwina takes my good elbow and guides me back to the bedroom. There is a cloudy mirror, cloudier now with condensation, hung on a nail above Celia's dresser. Edwina takes the chair from Celia's desk and positions it in front of the mirror, then motions for me to sit down. She drapes the damp towel around my neck, then grabs a comb and holds it inches above my head. "Right or left?"

"I'm sorry?"

"Do you part your hair on the right or on the left?"

"Oh." I squint at myself in the mirror, a small figure made smaller by her square-shouldered form, stationed sentry-like behind me. "Near the middle, but slightly to the left and a bit off-center. It should fall right into place."

She nods and combs my hair straight back off my face, then pushes it forward, looking for the natural part. "Well, well," she says mischievously, "one rarely sees this."

"What?"

"Dark hair with light roots."

"I'm naturally blond," I explain.

"Why the change?"

"I needed a new literary identity. Dayle Salvesen, unsuccessful but serious blond novelist, became Candee Cronin, best-selling brunette and author of the *Assignment* novels."

"Do you like the darker color?"

I shrug. "I'm used to it now. But it was weird, at first. When I saw my reflection in a mirror, I didn't always recognize myself."

Edwina parts my hair several times without satisfaction, then impulsively grabs the towel from around my neck and rubs my hair wildly, sending it flying in several directions. As she combs it neatly back into place, her gray eyes soften.

"What's wrong?" I ask.

"Nothing." She presses the edge of the comb against her generous bottom lip.

"Why are you looking at me like that?"

She glances down, shaking her head. "I didn't notice until just now how much you look like my Celia," she whispers. "Without makeup and with your hair combed back, there's such a strong resemblance." Her hands float slowly around my face, pausing to highlight each feature. "Same high cheekbones, thin eyebrows, narrow chin." She leans forward, nearly brushing my ear with her lip as she scrutinizes my reflection. "Your eyes are blue and hers are hazel, but the shape of the eyelid is similar. Dayle, you could be sisters."

I want to reply but my throat is too tight to speak as I stare into the mirror at the solemn, pale, reflected face, which at the moment appears to be Celia's. My gaze rises from my own face to Edwina's behind me and I see that she is weeping, silvery tears that course silently down the high tan planes of her face. Edwina weeps because she misses Celia, and I cry too, but not because of Celia, or even because of my son. I cry because it has been so long since anyone touched me with such kindness, such casual compassion, as Edwina does now, with one hand squeezing the comb and the other cupped softly at the base of my skull.

❖

After Edwina helps me change into my clothes for the lecture, an off-white silk Gucci blouse with navy blazer and skirt, she putters in the kitchenette, making tea, while I sit before the mirror and apply my makeup with one hand. The radio drones softly in the background, Top 40 pop music and inane call-in conversation, but at the top of the hour the tone turns serious with an updated news report about the ongoing fears of an imminent terrorist attack. *And in more local news,* the reporter continues, *the body of a young woman has been found dead near Waterloo Bridge. Police have yet to release the woman's identity.*

My whole body goes numb as Edwina lets out a strangled cry, doubling over as if she's been punched. I want to go to her and hold her up before she collapses, but I can't move. I feel like a rag doll, limbless and unhinged.

"God! Celia. No," Edwina coughs out between sobs.

"It might not be her," I say in a strange voice that sounds brittle and distant. "I'll call Callaway."

Moving across the room, I reach for the phone on Celia's desk but my hand shakes so badly I have to sit down and hold the phone in my lap, trying to keep it still. Twice I punch the wrong numbers and must hang up and try again.

At last Callaway's phone rings and goes straight to voice mail. I swallow hard, struggling to speak. "DC Callaway? This is Dayle Salvesen. We just heard on the news about...the woman. Near the river. Is it Celia?" My voice cracks. I take a deep breath and exhale. "I'm at Celia's flat with Edwina. Please let us know."

I put down the phone and stand, finding the strength to go to Edwina, who is still crouched at the sink, head bowed, dish towel wrapped around fists that have turned marble-cold and a bloodless white. "It's okay," I whisper, taking the towel and helping her stand. She is trembling and in shock: eyes hollow, pupils fixed. I take her elbow and guide her to Celia's stacked mattresses, where we sit, side by side. "It's okay," I say, stroking her back and patting her hand.

"She's gone," Edwina whispers between sobs. "Celia's gone."

"I know," I reply, not believing it.

"My sweet, beautiful girl is gone."

"I know." I close my eyes as the room goes dark, and deep in the recesses of my mind a wisp of an image stirs, collects itself, and assumes the physical form of Cecelia Frost. Celia the liberator, the freer of souls, being ferried across a river to safety on the other side. A boat slices through the mist, piloted by a ghostly boatman rowing steady, empty, even strokes, parting the fog in order to ease Celia's passage. All those she freed, the desperate and downtrodden, assemble on the opposite bank to welcome her into their fold, waiting with a feast prepared especially for her.

"We have to believe that she is free," I tell Edwina, feeling the weight of her head against my temple as her helpless body collapses at my side. "She's safe, and no one can hurt her now."

CHAPTER TEN

Wednesday
6:06 p.m.

Suddenly the phone rings and Edwina and I both jump. I can feel her heart hammering through her back as my own heart explodes in my throat. "Must be Callaway," I whisper.

I rise from the bed and stumble the few steps to Celia's desk. Fingers shaking, I grab the phone, nearly dropping the receiver. As I press the phone to my ear, I hear only my own rushing blood. I sit down quickly at Celia's desk and try to catch my breath. "Hello?"

"Dayle? Glad I caught you."

"Mom?" I ask hoarsely.

"Yes, hon. You're probably getting ready for your conference, but I'm calling to see if Celia's all right."

"What?" My head spins.

"I'm here at the condo feeding your cats and there's a message from Celia on your answering machine, asking you to call her right away."

I swallow hard before speaking. "Mom, I've got some bad news. We think Celia killed herself this morning."

"Good Lord! What happened?"

Struggling to think clearly, I quickly summarize what we know, and then ask, "What time did Celia leave that message?"

"What time?"

"Yes. It might be important."

"Just a sec." I hear her press the message button on the answering machine, followed by the drone of a distant mechanical voice, and somewhere, farther off, the frantic disembodied voice of Cecelia Frost, begging me to get in touch.

"Yesterday afternoon, 4:07," Mom repeats. "Isn't that right after you left for the airport?"

"Yes." My mind races. "I left at quarter to four—4:07 Chicago time would have been a little after ten p.m. in London. What else did her message say?"

"Nothing. Just that she wanted you to call her right away. She sounded terrified."

"Did she leave a number?"

"Yes." My mother repeats the number but I'm too addled to follow.

"Hang on a minute." I hold my hand over the receiver and call to Edwina, "Is your cell phone close by?"

Still sitting slack shouldered and hollow eyed on the bed, she nods robotically.

"Dial this for me." I return to my call. "Mom, give me that number again."

I repeat the numbers slowly. Edwina punches the digits into her cell phone and then presses it to her ear.

Suddenly my backpack begins to vibrate. Edwina's face drops. "My God," she gasps.

I reach into my backpack and pull out the phone—the one that had been stashed behind Celia's bed earlier in the day.

"Dayle! What is it?"

"It's okay, Mom," I say, turning off Celia's cell phone mid-ring. "That number is for a new cell phone with a foreign area code that I found stashed behind Celia's bed. Celia wanted me to call her back on this number. But she obviously didn't have this phone with her when she last left here."

"Baby, you need to come home," Mom says in a voice weak with worry. "Please come home."

"I will. After my speech. I'm booked on a flight tomorrow afternoon." I glance at the clock. "I need to go. I'll call if there's any news."

"Honey, please be careful."

"I will. I love you, Mom."

"I love you too."

I hang up the phone and look at Edwina. Some of the color has returned to her face as she stares at the cell phone clutched in her hand. "The number I dialed—the country code is Ireland," she says softly.

"Ireland?"

She nods. "Yes. I presented a paper at Trinity College last year and made several calls while there. That's the country code—353. Celia's phone was registered in Ireland."

"Does Celia have business there? Friends? Contacts?"

Edwina shakes her head slowly, squinting into the distance. "None, so far as I know. I don't believe she's ever even been there on holiday."

"She must have planned to go to Ireland sometime soon. When I arrived this morning, I found maps of Dublin and the DART here on Celia's desk." I press my good hand against the metal surface. "It can't be a coincidence, the cell phone and maps both connected to Ireland."

"Should we ring Callaway?"

I sigh. "No. Not now. Let's wait for her to get back to us about...you know." I can't bring myself to say the words.

"You're *still* going to the conference?"

"Yes. I have to." I rise from Celia's desk and my knees nearly give out beneath me. I grab my backpack, dump the contents onto Celia's kitchen table, and stuff a few key items— my wallet, lipstick, cell phone, business cards, ballpoint pen— into my attaché case.

"You're leaving those behind?" Edwina nods at Celia's wad of cash, the Marguerite Alderton credit card, and the ferry ticket still on the table.

"Yes. They're safer here."

"How do you reckon? The flat was ransacked."

"Exactly," I explain. "Whoever turned the place over didn't find the items. So, believing they aren't here, there would be no point in searching the flat again."

She sighs. "I suppose that makes sense."

Edwina phones for a taxi and we head downstairs to wait on the front steps of the building. It's twenty after six and the last light of day fades in the western sky as streaks of powder blue and pink bleed through the semisolid curtain of faceless gray. The last light of day, a day whose end Cecelia Frost did not live to see. All the days that still lie ahead and she will not be any part of them; she will never know about anything that happens from now on.

Edwina stands stiff backed beside me, heaving silent tears that gather at her jaw before dropping solidly onto her collar. I have no idea what to say. Traffic up and down Rosslyn Hill is steady as headlight after headlight blinks to life, illuminating the rain-slicked pavement and throwing dancing half-circles and shimmering crescents of light that burn brightly for an instant before they soften and die.

"Will you be okay?" I finally ask. "Is there someone you can stay with tonight?"

She brushes her cheek and jaggedly inhales. "My brother Julian lives in Peckham."

"Good." Before I can say more, the taxi arrives, screeching stiffly to a halt just before the curb. We walk down the steps and Edwina opens the door and helps me in. Once I'm settled into the backseat she passes me my attaché case, carefully avoiding my injured hand.

"Be brilliant," she says, propping open the door, leaning in, and forcing a brave smile. "That's what Celia would have wanted."

"I'll do my best," I whisper in reply.

Edwina closes the door with a muffled thud and I feel the echo somewhere deep within my broken metacarpal.

"Where to, miss?" the driver asks, glancing in the rearview mirror. He is a fiftysomething East Asian with large dark eyes and slicked-back hair trimmed neatly above his collar.

"Dartmouth House. Thirty-seven Charles Street, Mayfair."

"Oh, very posh, miss," he pronounces, raising his chin and smiling so I can see the brilliant reflection of his teeth.

He jackrabbits into traffic and I tumble back into the seat. I should review the notes for my speech but I'm still numb, trying to comprehend that Cecelia Frost is gone, that I will never again see her face or hear her voice. Mostly I want to say a prayer for her soul and ask her to look after my Rory, but Celia would despise such soft sentimentality; to her, life was for the living and death was just plain death, the end of everything. *The rest is silence*, as she liked to quote.

Suddenly the driver slams on the brakes and curses beneath his breath. He glances nervously in the rearview mirror and apologizes profusely, but I catch the intensity in his eyes.

"Is something wrong?" I ask.

"No, I am certain it is nothing," he reassures me.

I turn quickly and gaze straight into the penetrating headlights of a large white van creeping closer to our back bumper. Visible in the front seat are the silhouettes of two broad-headed, square-shouldered men. *No*, I think. *Please, no.*

Chapter Eleven

Wednesday
6:29 p.m.

"I need your help," I tell the driver, trying not to panic. "I think I'm being followed."

His black eyebrows, reflected, rise above the upper edge of the rearview mirror. "Is it the paparazzi?"

Paparazzi? Who does he think I am? "No, but I may be in danger," I say quickly. "Can you lose the van behind us?" The hot yellow lights of the vehicle burn into the back of my head, then creep over my shoulder and circle my throat.

This part of London, full of quiet, tree-lined suburban streets, does not offer much opportunity for evasive driving maneuvers, but the cabbie surprises me by turning off Belsize Avenue, barreling through an intersection and zigzagging up and down a number of side streets and narrow residential lanes before slipping into a steady stream of evening traffic moving through Swiss Cottage, heading south into the city. I turn, cup my good hand against the back window, and peer out to see if we're being followed. We aren't.

"How did I do, miss?" the cabbie asks breathlessly as we careen down Finchley Road.

"Great," I reply. "Actually, that was impressive."

"Yes, very cloak-and-dagger," he agrees, sounding satisfied as we resume a normal speed. Of course super-spy Redleigh Smith is an expert defensive driver. In *Assignment: Khartoum* she commandeers a Mini Cooper and races across a Sudanese sand dune littered with land mines while simultaneously dodging machete-wielding elements of the militant Janjaweed.

❖

There is no sign of the white van as the cab stops in front of Dartmouth House, the headquarters of the English-Speaking Union. The building is a large, luxurious Georgian town house located just southwest of Berkeley Square in the heart of Mayfair, one of the most exclusive areas of central London. After paying the driver I rush through the entrance's imposing marble columns, beneath two flags, the Union Jack and the St. George's Cross, and into the dazzling lobby. Once the doors are safely closed behind me, I peer through the glass and look up and down the street as I wait to catch my breath. Nothing. I'm just being silly. I probably only imagined I was being followed.

I turn around and proceed farther into the crowded lobby, where I am greeted by a large easel holding a placard with my black-and-white book jacket photo, blown up to enormous proportions, above big block letters that announce my keynote address.

I glance at my watch: 6:55. I was supposed to be here by 6:30. I'm almost half an hour late. I leave my coat at the coat check and as I thread my way through the elegant lobby jam-packed with conference attendees, my broken hand wakes with pain, seizing in response to the slightest brush of passing fabric. I wish I had the paracetamol that the nurse at the hospital recommended. My nerve endings are raw, constricting in anticipation as people barrel past me, some clutching books or bottled water, others attempting to lasso stacks of loose papers.

Suddenly Felicity Marchman, the conference organizer, pinpoints me in the crowd. I recognize her from her photo on the conference website. "Candee Cronin!" she bellows, rushing toward me. "We were worried you'd never get here. No one was even certain whether your flight had landed."

Damn. I was supposed to phone the organizers as soon as I arrived in London. They had disapproved of me flying in on the day of the conference and now, apparently, I have lived up to their lowest expectations.

"My goodness—what have we here?" Ms. Marchman's gaze sweeps broadly across my body, from shoulder to shoulder, and lands, horrified, on my left arm. "You appear to have some sort of...*injury*." She draws out the word injury as if I've committed a serious social faux pas by appearing in public with a plaster cast on my wrist.

"Yes." I slip the arm with the cast behind my back, out of sight. "An accident at Tottenham Court Road."

Her round, florid face betrays no sympathy as she withdraws a sheet of paper from the folder she is holding and thrusts it toward my shoulder. "Here is the conference agenda. *We've* been at it since nine a.m., you know. Of course you weren't here for the afternoon sessions. Beatrice Allenby's presentation on Taking Your Passion into Print was especially well received."

Beatrice Allenby—I recognize the name. Her first novel, a roman à clef about a young intern's affair with a Cabinet minister, has caused quite a stir. A recent graduate of the

University of East Anglia's creative writing program, Beatrice is the London literati's flavor of the month, complete with model-quality good looks and a suitably tragic backstory. Celia and I were once flavors of the month, it occurs to me, but that was years ago now.

I excuse myself from Ms. Marchman and make my way up the French marble staircase to the upstairs rooms, where the conference sessions are held. It feels like I've stepped back in time to an era of smoking jackets, gentlemen's clubs, and big-game hunters as I admire the rooms' rich tapestries, heavily draped curtains, marble fireplaces, and glittering chandeliers.

I step into the Small Drawing Room, where dozens of conference attendees mingle in small groups as the well-groomed waitstaff circulates with trays of hors d'oeuvres, canapés, and tea sandwiches. Just as I grab a flute of champagne from a tray held aloft by a young man in a tuxedo, a deep voice behind me suddenly calls out, "Dayle?"

I turn quickly. The voice belongs to Alec Stinson, the commissioning editor at Grenville & Howe Publishing who bought the rights to publish my first novel, *Down on Euclid Avenue*, while I was still in graduate school. Alec was always a good friend to me and a staunch supporter of my career when I lived in England. Although he knew I preferred women, he never gave up hope of making me one of his inevitable conquests.

"Alec?" I haven't seen him since a conference in Paris three years ago, but time has been kind. Always a handsome man, he is now, in his midfifties, more dashing than ever: still trim, with streaks of silver in his smooth black hair, tanned olive skin, and lines of emphasis around his deep green eyes. He is impeccably dressed in a dark Savile Row suit with a red-and-gold striped tie and crisp white shirt beneath.

He strides closer and opens his arms. "So lovely to see you," he booms in his rich baritone. "I was thrilled when I heard you'd be speaking tonight." He stops short of embracing me, noticing the cast on my wrist. "Oh, dear—what happened?"

"Tripped at the Tube station. Tottenham Court Road." I feel my face redden as I try to hide my arm. "You know me, always a klutz."

"Well, thank goodness it wasn't worse." Alec gently slides his palm down my good arm, ending with a lingering squeeze of my fingers. His touch, unexpected but not unwelcome, makes me want to cry. *Don't tell him about Celia. If you do, you'll break down.*

"You certainly look lovely." He smiles, pushing the hair back from my cheek. "The darker color really suits you."

"Thank you." The warmth of his hand makes me tingle.

"Have you been back in London long?" He frowns. "And why didn't you ring me so we could meet for our customary tea at The Savoy?"

"I only arrived this morning." I force myself to smile, even as my knees tremble and the walls seem to close in on me. "Alec, would you mind if we went someplace quieter?"

"Of course not. Perhaps there?" He gestures toward an unoccupied table draped with a long white cloth, on the noisy room's perimeter. I nod and he guides me to it with his hand on the small of my back.

"Better?" he asks hopefully, assuming a place at my side.

"Yes. Much," I reply.

"So, are you working on a new book?" He steps closer and holds me in his steady gaze.

I nod, relieved to be away from the heat and noise of the crowd. "Yes. *Assignment: Tokyo.* I'm going to Japan next month for research."

He offers a sly smile. "And what does our intrepid heroine get up to this time around?"

"Uncovers a plot by renegade Japanese scientists to steal nuclear secrets and frame the North Koreans."

Alec skeptically raises an eyebrow.

"Don't scoff," I protest. "Redleigh finally shows some character development by reconciling with her long-lost father."

"Ah yes, I remember." Alec lifts his chin and squints into the distance. "Wellington Peregrine Smith III. Wasn't he an international diamond thief who supposedly plunged to his death off Cap d'Antibes?"

I'm both shocked and flattered that Alec would recall such a minor detail from the first *Assignment* novel. "That's right. But of course he only staged his death to throw off Interpol."

"Quite. And are you working on anything else?"

The question surprises me. "*Assignment: Tokyo* isn't enough?"

"As Dayle Salvesen, I mean. A new book under your own name."

I shake my head. "No."

He looks away. "That's a pity, given your estimable talent."

I shrug. "Well, no one reads Dayle Salvesen's books. She's retired forever, I'm afraid." I'm about to say more when the room starts spinning and my knees weaken. Seeming to sense that I'm about to fall, Alec slips his arm around my waist and helps me to a nearby sofa, then crouches before me, stroking my hand.

"It's all right," he says gently. "Stay here—I'll fetch some water."

"No, wait. Don't go." I grab his hand. "I'm fine. I just need a minute." I bow my head, waiting for the room to stop rocking. I feel like I'm imploding, toppling inward toward a cold dark core.

Suddenly a large, disheveled man in an ill-fitting suit blunders toward me, nearly tripping over both his shoes and his words as he presses Candee Cronin for an autograph.

"*Assignment: Bangkok* is my favorite!" he blurts out, shoving a book beneath my nose. "I don't even mind if *Sao Paolo* isn't as good. I'm certain to love it anyway."

Alec rises and touches the man's arm. "If you don't mind, sir, now is not a good time," he says, firmly but politely. "She's feeling unwell. Perhaps after her speech."

"Oh. All right." The man nods and ambles away looking disappointed.

"Thanks for running interference on my behalf," I say as Alec's attention returns solely to me.

"It's my pleasure." He bends closer and peers into my face. "Shall I call for help?" he asks softly.

"No, it's okay," I reassure him. "It's just been a really rough day."

He grabs a nearby chair and sits down facing me, knee to knee. "Tell me—what's happened?"

I look up into his anxious green eyes and long to tell him everything. There is so much Alec doesn't know about the past three years. He never knew I was pregnant, and that I had, and lost, a baby. Suddenly I want to talk about Rory; I long to speak my child's name aloud and know that someone who cares about me has heard it. I want to describe how, after losing my son, I discovered within me a new place for pain to come from. I want to say all these things, but when I open my mouth something very different emerges. "Remember my flatmate, Cecelia Frost? The author?"

"Of course." He frowns, searching his memory. "*West of...*?"

"*West of Blessing, North of Hope.*" I pause. "Well, she died this morning."

"My God! What happened?"

"It seems she jumped off Waterloo Bridge."

"I'm so sorry, Dayle. I know you two were quite...close."

I bow my head and rub my temple. "I still can't believe it. When I arrived this morning, I heard that she was missing but only learned an hour ago that she had died."

He offers a gentle smile. "It was brave of you to come to the conference after getting such news."

"I had to," I explain. "Everyone was expecting me." I pause, looking around the shimmering drawing room. "Or I guess I should say, expecting Candee Cronin."

"Brave, nonetheless. Where will you go after?"

I take a deep breath and exhale slowly. "I had planned to stay with Celia, at her flat."

"Well, you won't want to stay there now. Come back to my place and rest."

I shake my head. "Thanks for the offer, but my luggage is at Celia's, and I've already booked a flight home for tomorrow afternoon. And I have to see Edwina."

"Edwina?" His face registers mild panic at the unfamiliar name.

"Celia's girlfriend. I need to say good-bye."

"Of course. But do you at least have time for a drink afterward?" He looks hopeful. "A number of us are meeting at The Only Running Footman, a nice pub just up the road. It would be lovely if you'd join us."

"Let's see how I feel." I offer a halfhearted smile. "My wrist and hand really hurt."

Before I can continue, Felicity Marchman's voice, amplified by a scratchy microphone, booms through the room. "Could I have everyone's attention, please?" She pauses. "Would our keynote speaker kindly approach the podium? I believe our other featured authors are already seated here behind me..."

"I have to go," I tell Alec. "Ms. Marchman clearly despises me."

"Dayle, no one could despise you." Alec winks, then his expression turns serious. "Are you certain you're up to this? Because if you aren't, I can let them know—"

"I'll be fine."

He smiles. "Well at least allow me to escort you to your seat."

His offer surprises me, but I comply. He helps me stand, and once I'm steady on my feet he leads me from the Small Drawing Room through the Long Drawing Room and into the Churchill Ballroom, a glorious, 1000-square-foot space resplendent with rich, dark Louis XIV walnut paneling, a gleaming wooden floor, and enormous chandeliers dripping with crystal. This is a room where I imagine serious things taking place—kingdoms divided, treaties signed, monarchs usurped.

High-backed wooden chairs are arranged in a row behind two long tables and a podium, where Felicity Marchman stands, square shouldered, just before the enormous marble fireplace featuring a roaring fire of orange and amber flames. The long tables are manned, I quickly realize, by the seven other authors who have presented at today's conference, including Beatrice Allenby, who sits on the far end in her size

2 Prada suit and looks bored as she tosses her head, running her manicured nails through her sheaves of long blond hair.

Alec walks me to the first empty seat behind the table and holds out his hand for support as I sit heavily, slightly off balance due to my cast. He bends to whisper in my ear. "If you need anything, just nod. I'll be right in front." I smile my thanks, then glance at Felicity Marchman, who eyes me icily.

I barely have time to settle myself and clear my head before I'm called to speak. One moment Ms. Marchman is introducing me as American novelist Candee Cronin, author of the bestselling *Assignment* novels, and the next I am standing behind the podium, staring out at an attentive crowd of around 250 mostly middle-aged men and women who breathlessly await my first words.

Celia should be here tonight. That's how I pictured it, as soon as I accepted the conference invitation. Celia sitting in the front row, rolling her eyes, desperate for a cigarette, stretching her arms and pantomiming a yawn. I would have had to cajole her to come, of course. She would not have wanted to seem too outwardly supportive or anything. Yet behind my back she would have been telling everyone at the conference how brilliantly subtle *Assignment: Sao Paulo* really is; deconstructionist and self-referential, she would call it, with faint yet palpable echoes of John Le Carré and Graham Greene.

I clear my throat and begin. "In *Mrs. Dalloway, To The Lighthouse,* and other works, Virginia Woolf gave us some of the greatest literature, not just by a female author, but by any author, of the twentieth century. And yet I propose that if Virginia Woolf were alive today, she would not be penning the character-driven literary fiction for which we remember her;

no, she would instead be creating GBLTQ romances and other genre works…"

When I finish speaking the audience politely applauds while Alec winks his approval from his seat in the front row. Following some brief closing remarks, Felicity Marchman announces that Beatrice Allenby will be signing copies of her novel during a wine-and-cheese reception in the Small Drawing Room. Yes, it occurs to me, Beatrice Allenby is this month's flavor. Candee Cronin is already fading; she will be a has-been soon enough. The fourth book in the *Assignment* series did not sell as well as the third.

In the ensuing orderly stampede of busy feet to meet Beatrice at the wine and cheese, I manage to lose myself in the crowd. Suddenly I catch a glimpse of Alec across the room with a tall, elegant brunette, midtwenties, at his side. His arm is around her narrow waist and she casually touches his hand as they converse with another couple, a professional-looking man and woman, who stand close to them in a loose semicircle. All four lean forward as if conspiring, or sharing a provocative joke.

I slip back into the crowd and follow the flow of people down the marble staircase and back to the lobby. I decide not to meet Alec and his colleagues at The Only Running Footman. My hand and wrist pulse with pain, and I doubt I'd be much fun.

I grab my coat from the coat check and hurry outside, where the temperature seems to have dropped fifteen degrees. My breath is visible and there is a suggestion of snow in the air, or perhaps, more accurately, it is a frosted fog that twinkles on the pavement, thickening my eyelashes and stiffening my collar.

I hurry across Charles Street, dodging sleek motorcycles and massive city buses, hoping to remain unseen by any departing conference attendees. Once across I hail a taxi and settle in for the ride back to Hampstead. I pull out my cell phone and check my voice mail. No messages from Callaway. As I return the phone to my attaché case, I release a deep breath. Now what? I dread the thought of returning to Celia's flat, to her little room with its makeshift bed, where only her ghostly aroma awaits to keep me company, along with the stale memory of a million smoked cigarettes, and the old mattresses that spread softly, ready to welcome the gentle pressure of her drowsy limbs. *At least when you get there,* I tell myself, *you can give in to grief. Once inside, no one can see you cry.*

❖

The taxi driver drops me in front of Celia's building, and after I pay him, he screeches away, leaving me marooned on the curb. An icy wind rises at my back as a loose paper wrapper cartwheels across the pavement near my feet. I turn and stare up at the front of the three-story Victorian structure. Its features appear sharper at night, more defined, as if carved from stone, with narrow, recessed windows and a solitary light on upstairs, in what must be the flat directly above Celia's.

I make my way up the front steps and push the door with my shoulder. It doesn't budge, so I push harder, until I realize the door is locked. This is the first time today that it's been locked. Perhaps they always lock the front door at night, or maybe word has gotten out that Celia's flat was ransacked and the tenants are suddenly more crime conscious. I glance at my watch: 8:30 p.m. Seeing no other option, I ring the buzzer for

Dot Crawford's flat, number 8, and hope that she is still awake and will buzz me in.

While I wait, I hear footsteps behind me, footsteps that pick up speed as they move closer. As I turn, the footsteps mount the steps and what there is of streetlight is suddenly blocked by two enormous figures, one on my left and one on my right. Before I can scream, or make any sound at all, a large hand is clamped across my mouth. *Dot*, I think. *Please open the door. Open it now.*

Chapter Twelve

Wednesday
8:32 p.m.

I'm too stunned to scream for help as the two burly men frog-march me down the concrete steps and bundle me into the backseat of an idling van, then whip the door closed with an angry rattle that splits the silence of night. I land on my left side, pinning my broken hand beneath me. A stabbing pain shoots up my arm and momentarily stops my heart as the van peels away down Rosslyn Hill.

"Who are you? What do you want?" Able to breathe again I sit forward and speak slowly, trying to disguise my rising terror. There are two men in the front, one in either seat. Both are broad shouldered and heavyset, with the passenger inches shorter than the driver and wearing a black fedora.

The driver glances at me in the rearview mirror. He has dark, deep-set eyes that suddenly, passing beneath the slivered light of a solitary street lamp, appear to be Polynesian. Oh no.

We are heading south, back toward the center of London. I search the horizon for a stoplight that might turn red in my favor, allowing me a chance to escape. Silently I reach for the door handle but just as my fingertips touch the cold metal, I hear the solid *click* as every door automatically locks.

"Please. Who are you? What do you want?"

No response.

We turn left onto a narrow, deserted side street off of Chalk Farm Road. The driver slows to a crawl behind a half-completed building site bookended by an empty parking lot and a row of industrial Dumpsters. Shadows gather and merge, creating overlapping layers of darkness with only thin fingers of light bleeding through from the street. Quietly unzipping my attaché case, I slip my hand inside and feel for my cell phone.

Suddenly the driver hits the brakes and pulls up short against a curb of crumpled pavement. The passenger, turning quickly in his seat, grabs the case from my lap and whisks it into the front seat, sending several items flying—lipstick, Kleenex, ballpoint pen.

"Don't be frightened," he says brusquely, in an accent I can't identify. "We won't hurt you. We just need your help."

"My help?"

Neither man answers as the van lumbers slowly away from the curb, threading the length of the side street before returning to Chalk Farm Road. I try to stay calm and focused. I've already made a potentially fatal mistake, allowing them to abduct me from outside Celia's flat and take me to a second location. And yet, if they wanted me dead, why not kill me at the building site and leave my body there?

I consider what Redleigh Smith would do under these circumstances. Kung fu, no doubt, with a few karate chops to the throat after momentarily mystifying her captors with an encyclopedic knowledge of conversational Samoan, complete with perfect noun declensions. Why did I write such rubbish? I suddenly wish Candee Cronin had never been born.

The men don't seem concerned that I can see them, viewing their faces in profile when we pass beneath streetlights. They might be brothers, both dark haired and olive skinned, mid-to-late thirties, with the smaller one likely younger by three or four years. They must mean to kill me. Otherwise they would hide their identities.

"You said you needed my help," I offer carefully, trying not to sound terrified. "What can I do?"

"You'll see," the driver says.

"Be quiet," the other one warns. "It won't be much longer."

A bolt of fear slices through me. I try to pray but I can't find the words. My mind races. Random images shuffle like a deck of cards across my consciousness, finally settling on the memory of my dead father, which rises to the surface and obliterates all other thought. My kind and loving father who was lost on opening day of the gun deer season, sixteen years ago. He was far from home when it happened, cocooned among the slender birch and fragrant pine of the Chequamegon National Forest, on the edge of the Bad River Indian Reservation. His beloved Gordon Setter, Axel, was at his side, and he had just finished setting up his tree stand when an errant rifle shot split the frigid afternoon and entered his abdomen.

In my mind I have viewed the scene a thousand times, each time trying to imagine a different ending. Pappa, shocked, first by the ruptured silence and then by the shattering pain, sinks to his knees in the snow. He sways side to side, struggling to stand, before collapsing onto his back and staring up at the sodden gray-white horizon. Axel, panicked, circles and cries, sniffing the air and the ground and the wound, so Pappa pulls him close and comforts him, stroking his black-and-tan head and whispering to him in nursery-rhyme Norwegian.

We know that, though mortally wounded, Pappa did not die right away. But, perhaps sensing the extent of his injury, he also did not call for help. Instead he settled himself on the ground where he had fallen, straightened his long narrow legs, and arranged his clothing. He removed his blaze orange cap, packed it with snow, and wedged it behind his head, where it melted and refroze, icing his ears to the ground.

Axel, loyal to the end, stretched out beside Pappa, breathing against his ribs to keep him warm. Side by side they must have lain there, considering the featureless sky for as long as it took for the life to seep out of him. Man and dog watched silently as snowflakes forming high in the atmosphere tumbled to earth, gaining weight and dimension during their descent, only solid when they finally came to rest on Pappa's golden-blond eyelashes. With his final breath he pressed one hand to the red stain spreading steadily over his midsection and draped the other hand softly across his heart. I have often wondered whether his last thoughts were of us, my mother and me, that we'd be told by the park warden who found his body that he died looking satisfied, like a man at peace with the world.

No. I won't give up. I won't just lie down and die. If these men plan to kill me, they have to know what they're taking. I sit forward, slipping my shoulders and torso into the narrow space between the two front seats, balancing my broken hand in my lap.

"My name is Dayle Salvesen." My voice sounds strong and steady. "You may know that I'm American and that I'm a writer. But I'm more than that. I have family; I belong to people. I was someone's mother for fifty-three minutes." I pause. "My disappearance won't go unnoticed."

The men exchange sideways glances but neither says a word as central London looms into view. I continue. "I grew up in Green Bay, Wisconsin, on a street full of tumbledown, shanty-shaped taverns with neon beer signs in the windows and strings of twinkling Christmas lights on display all year round. The city itself is compact and opens into Lake Michigan like the sprung joint of a giant elbow. Drive any distance in any direction away from the lake and you will find endless acres of cornfields, dotted with dairy farms that have red wooden barns and tall silver grain silos.

"When I was young, my father was my favorite person. He was fair-minded and generous, even though he was given to quiet moods during which no one could reach him. He had grown up on Norway's Hardangerfjord and refused to admit how much he missed home. I was an only, but not lonely, child, a tomboy who refused to play with dolls, but I loved animals and had an enormous black-and-white rabbit named Duchess. I could see the Glory Road water tower in Ashwaubenon from my bedroom window, and it seemed so huge that I imagined it was visible to astronauts floating across the surface of the moon."

We cross Waterloo Bridge and the van turns onto Belvedere Road and slows, screeching to a halt beneath Hungerford Bridge, just before the Royal Festival Hall. The doors unlock and I am startled into silence. The driver keeps the engine running while the passenger opens his door and jumps to the ground, then a moment later slides open the back door and motions for me to get out. Apparently I don't move fast enough because he reaches in, grabs my good arm, and drags me from the backseat. I'm still trying to find my balance as he hands me my attaché case. "Our apologies," he mumbles as he climbs back into the front seat, closes the door, and they speed away down Belvedere Road.

I am shaking so hard I can't catch my breath. I must call the police. I am reaching into my attaché case and fumbling for my cell phone, barely able to see in the hollow brick cavern beneath the bridge, when a soft voice behind me calls out, "Wait."

I turn quickly and stare straight into the shadowy face of Cecelia Frost.

Chapter Thirteen

Wednesday
8:53 p.m.

"Celia—you're supposed to be dead," I whisper, choking on the words.

"We're not safe here—come, follow me."

She turns to flee but I reach out and grab her arm, spinning her around. "Wait." I step closer and stare into her half-hidden face. Without a doubt it is Celia, looking as she did in the photo that arrived this afternoon, drained and underweight with brittle, bleach-blond hair roughly cut and skimming her narrow shoulders. The only differences are a slightly blackened eye and an aging facial scar, curved and strangely elegant, an inverted pink smile bisecting her sunken left cheek. Dressed in faded jeans, scuffed boots, and a denim jacket over a dirty white T-shirt, she looks ruined: an anemic, jaundiced, malnourished mess. And yet she is also fantastically alive, with a nervous energy pulsing just beneath her skin, skin that is opaque and iridescent, as if beat to airy thinness, or hollowed by a flame of desperation.

"We have to go," she says roughly, "now." She jerks my good hand and the jolt electrifies my heart. Still dressed in my raincoat, skirt, blouse, blazer, and pumps, I struggle to keep pace as she darts along the damp thoroughfare of Belvedere Road, past a deserted parking lot on one side and faceless gray office buildings on the other. She turns onto a concrete path that cuts through the flat green expanse of the Jubilee Gardens, not even stopping for breath until we reach the approach to the massive London Eye, the huge Ferris wheel erected along the banks of the Thames to celebrate the birth of the new millennium. The Eye, which looks like an enormous bicycle wheel with long narrow spokes and glass-encased passenger capsules attached to its outside circumference, towers over central London's cityscape, dwarfing even Big Ben and the Houses of Parliament.

"Over here," Celia pants, nodding toward the ticket office inside the County Hall. "We're just in time for the night's last flight."

I follow her across the street and inside, struggling to catch my breath as I stand behind her in the ticket line. "Celia—the bridge, the body…"

"Shush!" She turns and scowls at me, pressing a finger to her lip.

"Sorry," I mumble, content now, given the brighter indoor lighting, to gaze at the back of Celia's neck, watching the muscles tighten and release as she purchases two tickets for the ride. I don't dare blink for fear she'll disappear. It occurs to me that I might be dead; perhaps the men in the van really did kill me and now it is only my soul that is coursing the damp concrete rise and fall of London's South Bank, trailing the elusive ghost of Cecelia Frost, whose death has a mere seventeen hours on my own. I don't care. I don't care at all. I am just so glad to see her.

The tickets purchased, Celia turns and beckons me to follow her back to the entrance of the Eye, up a wooden ramp, through a security checkpoint, and to the embarkation point on the very edge of the Thames where we stand, hunched against the cold, waiting for the next empty passenger capsule to reach us. The wheel moves continuously at a steady pace, but the movement is so slow that there is time enough to empty and refill each compartment without stopping the wheel. Normally the London Eye is overrun with tourists and a long line of people waits to board, but tonight the ride is nearly empty, no doubt due to the cold, the fog, and the lateness of the hour.

When our capsule arrives we step inside the glass-walled, oval-shaped, futuristic-looking pod, and an attendant closes the door behind us. The capsule, which is stationary save for the revolution of the wheel itself, is large enough to hold at least twenty people, but Celia and I have this capsule all to ourselves.

We rise slowly above the thick oily ripple of the Thames, watching it churn darkly beneath our feet. The glass capsule's normally panoramic view of late-night London's illuminated landscape is blurred by drizzle and softened by fog, leaving only the largest and brightest sights visible, poking through the gloom.

Suddenly the lights go down inside our pod, leaving nothing but a low blue glow. Celia takes a seat on the slatted wooden bench in the center of the capsule, where the muted light gently envelops her, erasing years from her appearance. She takes a deep breath and exhales slowly, as if releasing a huge weight. A slight nervous smile plays about her pale lips and her face becomes youthful again, almost impish, although the smile never reaches her eyes.

"Sorry for all the cloak-and-dagger," she says softly. "We can speak freely here. We have about thirty minutes until we once again touch ground." She pulls a crumpled pack of cigarettes from the breast pocket of her denim jacket and taps one into the palm of her hand. Of course smoking is not allowed inside the capsule, but Celia doesn't care.

"Celia, everybody thinks you're dead." Even in the semidarkness my eyes keep searching her face, looking for details, anxious for proof that she is real.

She clamps the cigarette between her teeth and grimaces. "I know. I wanted it to look that way."

"But the dead body...?"

Her eyes widen. "Dead body?"

"At Waterloo Bridge."

She shakes her head, pausing midshake to search for her lighter. "There was no dead body. I dumped my car near the bridge at four this morning so everyone would think I'd offed myself."

"But there was a report on the radio that police found the body of a young woman there this afternoon. We assumed it was you."

The cigarette ignites, the brief flash of ruby intense against the mellow blueness. She draws a deep breath, then exhales. "Clearly, it wasn't me. Must be a coincidence. It is a popular spot for suicides, after all." She pauses. "Dayle. I need your help."

"Help with what?"

"I must leave London."

"I figured that, but why?"

She squints, blowing a plume of smoke that, unable to escape the closed confines of the glass capsule, hangs heavily around her head. "You know that I work with girls, some so young they have yet to reach puberty, who are trafficked into the UK as prostitutes, sex slaves, and forced labor."

"Yes."

"Well, this multinational trade is primarily controlled by highly organized criminal gangs, many originating in Eastern Europe or affiliated with the Russian Mafia. My work sometimes cuts into their profits, but I'd always been able to negotiate with them."

My mind flashes back to what Callaway had said at the hospital, about Celia interacting with criminals. "What exactly do you mean by negotiate?" I ask carefully.

"Just that—negotiate," she snaps. "I can't go into detail, but suffice it to say, we had an agreement that allowed me to get some of the girls off the streets. But then about six months ago, things changed. The gangs began threatening me. Then the threats turned violent. They attacked me in the street last week—hence this." She indicates her damaged face with the filter end of the cigarette.

"So Edwina was right—the mugging wasn't random."

"No. I knew who attacked me but didn't dare tell the police."

"And that explains the photo."

"Photo?"

"In today's mail there was an envelope with a close-up photo of you, beneath which someone had scribbled, *We can make you disappear.*"

Her eyebrows rise. "Subtle, they are not."

"You've had other threats?"

She nods solemnly. "Several, in fact. Round Christmas I realized my life was in serious danger and I had no choice but to leave the country. So I invited you to visit, hoping you'd agree to help me build a new life in the States under my mother's name—Marguerite Alderton."

So that's why she wanted to see me. It was never just a friendly visit, ex-lovers hoping to catch up. "But then why dump the car last night, before I even arrived?"

She flicks a coil of cigarette ash to the capsule floor and grinds it beneath her heel. "Originally I thought we would stage my suicide sometime next week, after we'd had time to organize. I would sail to Ireland, then fly from Dublin to the States."

"Why the change of plans?"

"Last night one of the Russians threatened to kill me if I didn't pay them twenty-five hundred pounds by this afternoon, so I had to bring forward the faked suicide in order to buy some time."

My mind races as I struggle to take in the new details. "What time last night were you threatened?"

"Must have been half nine."

"And then you phoned my condo around ten p.m.—four p.m., Chicago time—and left that frantic message on my answering machine."

She nods. "Precisely. After my encounter with the Russian I couldn't return to the flat to get the things I need for Ireland— cash, clothes, mobile, ferry ticket. So this afternoon, when I saw you and Edwina leave, I sneaked into the flat and searched for the things, but they were gone. Dayle, where are they?"

"Back at your apartment." I draw a sharp breath. "*You* ransacked the flat."

"Yes. To cover my tracks. So you wouldn't guess I'd been there."

My head spins. Needing a moment to think, I step to the rounded front nose of the capsule, press my hands to the cold glass, and stare down at the dark dream vision of London glittering beneath me. We are near the top of the wheel now, more than 400 feet off the ground. The lumbering sky feels low and dolorous, dense with alternating shades of violet, black, and indigo, lightened only by the lacy wreaths of fog that grace the tops of the highest buildings. They say that on a clear day, from the top of the Eye one can see twenty-five miles, or as far as Windsor Castle. But tonight only a few key landmarks assert themselves through the gloom: Big Ben, the Houses of Parliament, the Ministry of Defence.

"Who are the men who brought me here?" I finally ask, my breath fogging the glass.

"Miko Tenuta and his younger brother, Temura. Associates from the antitrafficking world, protecting me from the gangsters." Celia pauses. "Supposedly, anyway."

I turn to face her. "Has Miko followed me all day?"

She stubs out her cigarette and then brushes the crushed butt to the floor, kicking it beneath the bench. "I don't believe so. I had him check this morning to confirm you'd arrived. Then he and Temura picked you up outside the flat after you returned from your speech."

"Did Miko follow me onto the train to Holland Park?"

"I don't think so." She pauses, looking concerned. "Holland Park?"

"I saw Dr. Whitaker."

"Why?" she asks warily.

"To figure out what the hell happened to you. Dot Crawford and Edwina said you'd attempted suicide twice, first slitting your wrists, then OD'ing on sleeping pills. But Fiona knew nothing about the overdose." I pause. "That's because it was faked, wasn't it?"

She considers lying to me; we both realize it at the same moment so instead she offers the truth. "*Faked* insofar as I didn't actually intend to end my life, yes."

"Why?"

She leans back on the bench, crosses her ankles, and folds her arms. "This goes back about two months," she explains. "I had already decided to leave England and start fresh in the States. I knew my supposed leap from Waterloo Bridge would be more credible if I'd twice attempted suicide in the previous year, the second time as recently as two months earlier. So I took enough pills to make me ill, but not kill me."

"And you didn't tell Dr. Whitaker because you knew she'd be suspicious."

She nods. "Precisely. Attempting suicide didn't fit the symptoms I was then experiencing."

"Was slitting your wrists fake too?"

She appears horrified. "God, no! To my great shame and regret, that attempt was legitimate."

When I don't respond, she searches my face anxiously. "You must believe me," she insists.

"I'm no longer sure what to believe," I admit.

"It's true. Dad's death left me gutted. He suffered so in his final months. I have devoted my life to helping those in need, but I could not help the one who mattered most." Her hard hazel eyes soften as she shakes her head. "Dayle, you would not have recognized him toward the end. Barely nine stone when he died, all his hair gone, his mouth and throat so full of sores he could not swallow."

Not for the first time in my life I am glad that my father died quickly, and where I could not see him. Pappa *was* thinking of us—my mother and me—when he died.

"It was a foolish, stupid, melodramatic gesture on my part." Celia uncrosses her arms and offers them as proof, palms up and wrists flexed. "Dad would have been furious, of course."

The pale skin of her wrists catches what little light there is inside the glass capsule and I step closer, peering down, but before I can get a good look she pulls away. "Wait," I say. "Let me see."

Warily she again presents her arms, wrists emerging slowly from the dark caverns of her denim sleeves. I sit down beside her on the bench, place her left palm in my lap, and carefully explore the scarred wrist with my fingertip. Celia shudders as I slowly trace the bubbled, uneven pink skin. Skin that was stitched quickly, artlessly, the only concern being to seal the slashed vessel and save her life. The damaged skin reminds me of a gash on canvas that destroys a work of art. This is really Celia here beside me, I think, and she is changed forever. She is no longer the same Celia I once made love to. I curl her fingers into a fist, which I squeeze with my good hand. *"Handle me and see,"* I whisper, *"for a spirit hath not flesh and bones as ye see me have."*

Celia stares steadily into my eyes, almost daring me to kiss her. I let her hand fall softly to her side, then return to the glass nose of the capsule.

"I haven't been up here for years," I whisper, looking down at the white steel girders that connect our pod to the outside of the wheel. Inside the pod just behind us I can make out the silhouettes of half a dozen people, some walking the perimeter of the capsule, others standing side by side. A man with his arm around a woman points out the sights as their wiry figures are intermittently illuminated by the flicker of a camera flash.

"It's still beautiful to me, the little we can see tonight," I continue. "It looks like a fairy tale down there—all the pleasure boats and barges slipping down the river, the rows of lights outlining the bridges and embankments. When I was a kid, I worried I would never see anything beyond the Glory Road water tower with *Ashwaubenon* written on the side in green and gold. To me that marked the outer edge of the possible world."

"London is a bloody nightmare," Celia complains, kicking out her heels. "Can't wait to be rid of this horrid place."

"How can you say that?" I challenge. "This is your home."

"Britain has changed since you last lived here. The country is falling apart, a casualty of the rampant consumerism that has reigned since Thatcher's tyrannical regime. All our major institutions are corrupt—government, education, the local authorities, right through to the legal system, the banks, the media. Our so-called leaders are inept, greedy, or incompetent. Sometimes all three. Being British used to mean something. It doesn't anymore. I'm ready to move on."

We are both quiet for a while, until I ask softly, "Was breaking up with Edwina also part of your plan?"

She pauses before replying. "You must know that it was."

"She's heartbroken."

"I had no choice."

"Why not?"

"I was leaving Britain forever. I figured it would be easier to accept my death if we were no longer a couple."

"She would support you, unselfishly, even at her own expense. Why not tell her the truth?"

"To protect her! Dammit, Dayle. If the Russians find out I'm still alive, even in the States, they could target her. The less Edwina knows, the better."

We're nearing the end of our journey through the London night sky and I struggle to recall everything I need to ask Celia. I sense that she will disappear the moment we touch ground. "The delivery," I say suddenly.

"Delivery?" she asks.

"Edwina and I saw Sophie Jameson at the hospital when I broke my hand. She said she expected you to make a delivery tonight. Perhaps money."

She nods. "That's right. My original plan, before I had to move up the staged suicide, was to give Sophie a going-away donation of twenty-five hundred pounds. For her shelter."

"Where would you get twenty-five hundred pounds?"

"From the five thousand I had stashed behind my mattress." She pauses. "Did you think I planned to take all of it with me to Ireland?"

"Well, yes," I admit. "That was everything you have."

"I only need twenty-five hundred. The rest was for Sophie. Although I don't know how I'll give it to her now." For the first time tonight, Celia's face shows real regret.

I stretch, raising my good arm above my head. "Celia, let's go back to your flat and get some sleep," I say. "I've booked a seat on a flight to Chicago tomorrow afternoon. I'll buy you a ticket too and we can go together."

She shakes her head. "I can't."

"Why not?"

"I can't travel as Cecelia Frost now that Cecelia is supposedly dead, and I don't have a Marguerite Alderton passport," she explains. "I've arranged to have one made in Dublin. I can get from here to Ireland with just an ID card, but without a passport I can't fly abroad."

"Oh."

"Dayle, that's why you have to help me."

"How?"

"Meet me at the Circle of Lebanon, Highgate Cemetery. The tomb of Radclyffe Hall. Quarter past nine. You'll find a bright red gym bag inside the wardrobe at my flat. Bring that, along with the cash, the clothes atop my suitcase, the ferry ticket, credit card, and mobile phone. There's a train tomorrow at ten past five in the evening, from Euston to Holyhead. I'll take that, then sail to Dublin and fly from there to the States. I'll contact you as soon as I'm settled."

"That sounds so risky," I argue.

"Please! It's the only way." She takes a deep breath. "I'm scared, Dayle. And I can't get out of London without your help."

I've never seen Celia so rattled. Always the queen of cool, she never loses her composure. "Of course. You can count on me," I reassure her. "I'll be there."

We watch as the pod just in front of us unloads its passengers. Then Celia and I take up position near the door to our pod, preparing to disembark. Standing beside Celia, our arms nearly touching, I can feel her anxiety rise the closer we get to the ground.

"Quarter past nine," she reminds me. "Don't forget my things."

"I won't."

An attendant opens the glass door and we step out onto the concrete platform as our pod continues on its journey, rising slowly behind us. "Don't tell Edwina or the police that I'm still alive," she warns.

"I won't."

We move quickly through the grounds of the Eye and enter the Jubilee Gardens. Celia's pace increases with each step. "Don't tell anyone that you've seen me."

"I won't." I want to grab her arm and hold on tightly, stealing a few final moments together.

"Please, Dayle. I'm counting on you." Her voice is frantic.

"Celia, you can trust me. I promise."

We reach Belvedere Road and stop to catch our breath. I turn to embrace her but she takes a step back and holds up her hand, palm outward. "Noli me tangere," she warns—*touch me not*. "Quarter past nine. The tomb of Radclyffe Hall. There'll be time for hugging then"—she grimaces—"if you insist."

And with that she turns and runs away, back through the Jubilee Gardens, swept up by the darkness of night: a shade, a slip, a shadow. I remain standing silently, cold and alone on this damp, deserted street, with the warmth of her presence cooling against my skin, her breath a memory lingering over my head, and that voice I was certain I'd never hear again still sounding in my ear. Celia. My darling Celia. Could it be? A death redeemed. And suddenly, nothing seems impossible.

CHAPTER FOURTEEN

Wednesday
9:34 p.m.

With Celia gone, I glance at my watch. A little after nine thirty. I have just under twelve hours until we meet again at the Circle of Lebanon. I haven't slept in a day and a half, haven't eaten since eleven o'clock this morning. My broken hand aches with a bone-deep pain and I am beyond exhausted. But Celia lives and breathes and walks the earth, a fact that, for the moment anyway, redeems all sorrows that ever I have felt.

It's a five-minute walk to Waterloo Station, through the concrete urban landscape of South London, where the darkened sky seems pierced, sectioned by bent metal cranes, and the girders, beams, and scaffolding of endless construction sites are soiled by street grime and runaway graffiti.

I enter the station and descend to the platform for the Northern Line, where a lone busker plays the guitar very badly and sings plaintively off-key, and the walls are plastered with ads for cheap overseas holidays and billboards for current West End plays, mostly recycled Broadway musicals.

I stand with my back to the station wall, close my eyes, and breathe in the trapped, drafty scent of emptiness that fills the Underground at night. At this hour a cold and filthy odor rises from every surface as the dirt and breath and dust and sweat accumulated throughout the day settle into permanence, pressing against the brick walls, conspiring beneath the platforms, tiptoeing along the tracks. But even this lonely, desperate, and despairing smell can't lessen the joy of having just seen Celia. I lean back and smile.

❖

When I enter Celia's ransacked flat, nothing appears changed since I left for the conference three and a half hours earlier, but the cramped, chaotic, and messy little room seems immediately different, revealing with a sly grin the secret it's been dying to tell me since I arrived this morning—that Cecelia Frost is still alive.

I change into a T-shirt and sweatpants, leaving my conference clothes in a heap beside the bed. As tired as I am, I am too wired to sleep just yet, so I put on one of Celia's favorite CDs, Van Morrison's *Veedon Fleece*, and listen as the warm, rich, throaty tones of the Belfast Cowboy fill the little room. I search the cabinets and find two bottles of wine, a cheap pinot grigio and a better merlot, along with a bottle of Glenfiddich scotch, three-quarters empty. I even manage to find and light two votive candles, which I place on the kitchen table as I pour myself a generous glass of merlot.

The achingly urgent falsetto of "Who Was That Masked Man" is just beginning and the merlot has sufficiently warmed my limbs when a tentative knock at the door startles me back to reality. Celia? I step to the unlocked door and grasp the handle, pressing it closed until I know for sure.

"Who's there?" I ask, trying not to sound scared.

"Dayle?"

For a moment I can't place the voice.

"Dayle—it's me. Edwina."

"Oh." I open the door. "Come in," I say softly, ushering her inside, where her large frame dominates the room. Edwina has changed clothes from earlier and now wears gray sweatpants, battered running shoes, a black leather jacket, and a man's navy-blue V-neck sweater with a white T-shirt beneath. Her lips and eyelids are creased and swollen and her dense hair is flattened on one side, making her look younger, loose jointed, and unkempt.

"I thought you were with your brother," I say softly. I can't look her in the eye without revealing that Celia is still alive.

She nods. "I was. And Julian was lovely. But I need to be here. Close to Celia. Close to her things." Her voice breaks as she draws a breath. "Sorry I didn't ring first. I wasn't sure if you'd be back yet."

"That's okay. I understand."

She drapes her leather jacket on the doorknob and I guide her to the kitchen table as I grab a second glass and turn down the music. "A drink?" As I raise the merlot, the bottle trembles. I am moments away from telling Edwina everything.

"Please," she replies with a nod. I pour her a glass and refill my own, then take the seat across from her at the kitchen table.

"How was the conference?" she asks.

"Good. Fine." I know I sound nervous. "I ran into my former editor, Alec Stinson. It was nice seeing him again."

"Celia had an editor on her last book." She smiles bitterly. "They did *not* get on."

"Yes. I remember. Daphne Quinn."

"It's overwhelming…"

"Yes?"

"How many people need to be told of Celia's death. I don't know where to begin."

"You don't have to worry about that tonight."

"I suppose not."

We both fall silent as Van Morrison sings softly in the background, barely audible. Edwina swirls her wine slowly, holding the glass by the stem and watching the dark red liquid lick the sides. She raises the glass to her lips but then sets it down without drinking.

"What do you think it was like?" she asks quietly.

"What?"

"When Celia died."

When Celia died? But she didn't. If only I could tell you. "I don't know." My glass quivers as I lift it to my lips.

"Do you think it was painful?"

"Not necessarily." I swallow, too quickly, and the wine sears my throat. "Compared to some deaths."

"But panicky." She sounds almost hopeful as the pupils of her large gray eyes capture the candlelight.

"Maybe."

"No, it would have to be," she insists.

"I suppose you're right." Please—let's change the subject.

She runs a thumbnail along a ridge in the kitchen table, pressing intensely until her nail turns white. "Have you ever been trapped underwater?"

This question surprises me. "No. Have you?"

She nods slowly, staring hypnotically at the candle. "Once. At a swimming pool. Someone jumped on my back and dunked me unexpectedly. It was brief, but horrible."

I can't stand this. "Edwina, maybe—"

"How could she?" Edwina looks up at me and her face collapses, paled by anguish. "I found her when she overdosed, you know. On the bathroom floor. Ashen. Barely breathing. When I lifted her, she vomited. I feared she might die in my arms."

Please stop. "Edwina…"

"And now I wish that she had." Her face suddenly hardens, triumphant with fury.

"Wish she had what?"

"Died in my arms."

"You can't mean that."

She nods vigorously, bottom lip firm. "I do. I'd rather she died in my arms than jumped from Waterloo Bridge. If I'd known at the time of the overdose that her life would end like this, I would not have saved her."

This is unbearable. "You couldn't have known this would happen," I argue.

"No? No?" She is nearly shouting now. "Celia attempted suicide twice, why not again? She obviously wanted to die."

"No one can know what she thought or felt in those harrowing moments." I take a deep breath and release it slowly. "But wherever she is now, at least she's free."

"It's so easy for you Americans to believe that." Her tone is bitter, accusatory. "Or at least pretend that you do." She pauses. "You can't possibly understand."

"Don't be so sure."

"Really?" she challenges.

"Really."

"You haven't lost the love of your life."

Haven't I? I choose my words carefully. "I don't believe in a hierarchy of grief. Pain is just pain, that's all." I pause. "But I have lost a child."

She looks up with a start. "My God. I had no idea."

"And he was the love of my life."

"What happened?" she whispers.

I stand, move across the room, and take a seat on Celia's stacked mattresses. I have no choice now but to tell Edwina everything. She rises from the table and comes to sit beside me. "Rory lived for fifty-three minutes," I begin slowly. "From 4:16 to 5:09 p.m., last October nineteenth."

I take a deep breath, rolling the wineglass between my palms. "Rory's father never even knew I was pregnant. Michael was in town for a photo shoot. We hadn't seen each other for a few years, so we had dinner, just to catch up, and one thing led to another. I don't often sleep with men, but it happens. I found out I was pregnant six weeks later. By then Michael was in Singapore, I believe."

"Wouldn't he have wanted to know?" Edwina asks gently.

I nod. "I planned to tell him. After the baby was born, I suppose. So he couldn't suggest an abortion."

"I see." Edwina folds her hands and wedges them between her knees.

"I never imagined myself having children, but suddenly I desperately wanted this baby," I continue, my thoughts far from London now. "I didn't mind being pregnant and on my own. I have the money, and my mother moved to Chicago to help out."

Edwina rapidly scans my face. "Dayle, what happened? What went wrong?"

"My placenta ruptured," I explain. "In the third trimester."

She frowns. "I'm not certain what that means."

I place my empty wineglass on the floor beside my foot. "It happens when the placenta, the organ inside the womb that supplies blood and nutrients to the baby, detaches from the wall of the uterus before it's supposed to. This causes massive blood loss for the mother and jeopardizes the baby's life."

"God." Edwina shivers. "How horrible."

"I was in surgery for hours and had no idea what was happening. When I woke up afterward and saw my mother's face beside me, I knew. Her eyes told me everything."

Edwina strokes my back gently, as if afraid I might shatter. "I'm so sorry."

I close my eyes and continue, speaking now from a place inside myself that is usually mute. "The doctors knew right away that they couldn't save him. So the nurses bathed him and washed his hair, then wrapped him in a blue-and-white blanket and placed him in my mother's arms. Mom had longed for him as much as I had. She had big plans for her grandson, but she put her hopes and dreams and grief aside and just held him, rocking him until he died.

"After I woke up from the anesthesia and was told he was gone, they wanted to bring him to me, but I said no. I didn't want to see what I had lost. I preferred to think of it as a miscarriage, a blob of tissue expelled by my body, not a real little boy who had lived for fifty-three minutes. But the hospital psychologist insisted. She said I would regret not saying good-bye and that my grief would be easier to process this way.

"So they brought him to me in my hospital bed, still swaddled in the blue-and-white blanket. He seemed so fragile as I unwrapped him, like a porcelain doll, but much more detailed, as if he'd been fashioned by a loving hand. Mom was beside my bed and we took turns holding him and hugging him and kissing him—I was still very weak, you see. To me he seemed flawless, with dimpled elbows and fat little feet. A cleft chin and full lips, fuller than I would have expected, like the petals of a rosebud, or a four-leaf clover.

"I could not believe my body had made something so beautiful. Rory had light brown hair, enough for me to comb with my fingers. His eyes were closed, of course, when he came to me, but Mom had seen his eyes open and she said he seemed to recognize her. Like he wanted to tell her something about his journey. His eyes were a beautiful pale blue, she said, exactly like my father's."

I look up and see tears streaming down Edwina's face, carving dark furrows into the smooth surface of her skin.

"I couldn't bring my son safely into the world." My voice breaks. "I gave him birth, yes, but not life, beyond those precious fifty-three minutes. I couldn't bring him into this world and I wasn't there to carry him into the next. I'm a failure. As a woman. As a mother."

"No. Don't say that." Edwina takes my face in her hands and stares into my eyes. "Please, don't. Your son's life was perfect, in its own way. He never felt scared or lonely or rejected. He was held and cherished and loved every moment of his fifty-three minutes on earth. How many people can honestly say that?"

"Maybe you're right." A sob flutters from my throat. "But I wanted a whole life for him instead."

Edwina wraps me in her arms and gently rocks me back and forth. "It's all right, love. It's all right," she says. Her voice is deep and soothing, slipping into my ear and, from there, shuttling into my bloodstream, which slows in response. I close my eyes and dissolve in her arms. It has been so long since I felt this, I think, pressing against her neck. Felt anything, really. But especially this. And there is a word for it: solace.

Edwina circles my torso and leads me to a safe place at her center. I surrender to a long-forgotten dream of comfort, letting it flash up and down my arms as my skin blisters and peels, revealing something fresh and pink and naked underneath.

"Shh, just relax," Edwina whispers in my ear. I raise my head and my lips brush her neck; before I know it, I am squeezing her shoulder. The muscles of her upper back tighten, solid as bedrock. She kisses my earlobe and a moan escapes her mouth as her bent knee seeks to separate my legs.

"Wait," I say suddenly, pushing her away. She pulls back in surprise as a torrent of blood rushes to her face.

"Sorry," she mumbles. "Sorry, sorry, sorry."

"No, it's all right." I reach for her hand but instead clasp only her first two fingers, which she quickly withdraws.

"No, it's not. I shouldn't have."

"Don't apologize. Really." I force a smile. "I'm flattered. But…"

"You're afraid we're betraying Celia." Her pale eyes are huge and wounded.

"No, it's not that. It's that I haven't been—haven't been close to anyone in months. Since before Rory was born." I stroke her arm, hoping she'll understand. "I'm just not ready yet."

"Can you believe me?" She gives a hollow laugh as her skin continues to darken, drenched with shame. "Celia not one day dead and I make a pass at her friend."

"Please don't say that. It's normal to reach out. Especially now." I lean close to touch her face but she pulls back and stands, weak-kneed, struggling for balance.

"This doesn't have to be awkward." I try to sound cheerful. "Come on, I think we could both use a drink." I stand, grab my wineglass, and shuffle to the kitchen table. My hand shakes as I reach for the bottle of merlot.

"Thanks, but I'd best be on my way." She hurries to the door, then grabs her leather jacket and fights it over her broad shoulders.

As I move toward her, she steps back. "Will I see you again before I go?" I ask softly.

"When do you leave?"

"Early tomorrow morning."

Still facing me, she reaches behind her back and feels frantically for the door handle, turning it slowly. "Hmm. I've got a class at nine. I'll phone you to say good-bye."

"Let me call you a cab." My voice sounds raspy and desperate. "You might wait awhile to catch one this time of night."

"No, that's fine." She slowly, silently, inches open the door and slips her foot into the hallway. "The night bus runs all hours."

"You don't have to go," I offer, but she is out the door before I finish the sentence. The quick patter of her running shoes picks up speed as she flies down the hall toward the staircase. "Edwina," I call after her, stepping into the corridor, desperate not to wake the neighbors. "Please come back. Please? Don't leave this way."

She doesn't respond; instead she simply disappears down the stairs. I turn back into the flat and close the door behind me.

With Edwina gone I feel utterly and completely alone, while the ghost of my lost child reverberates around the room, tormenting me with his presence. Now that his name has been released into this sad space, something of him remains, so close and yet impossible to see or touch or taste or feel. I fall facedown onto Celia's stacked mattresses and begin to pray:

And there went a man of the house of Levi, and took to wife a daughter of Levi. And the woman conceived, and bare a son.

In a matter of moments I am asleep and dreaming. In the dream I prepare to send Rory away, but first I must bathe him at the riverbank, because if he is clean and shiny and smells nice, whoever finds him on the other side will love him even more, hold him awhile longer, and salt his tender skin with kisses. I immerse him in the swift current, dunking him up to his tummy, as his chubby legs thrash madly in the rushing water, water whose warmth recalls a womb so recently vacated that it still holds his shape, still remembers his dimensions.

Once he is clean and dry, I dress him carefully in pajamas, socks, and mittens, and a white knit cap to cover his vulnerable crown, the breach in the bone that pulses steadily beneath his soft brown hair.

And when she could not longer hide him, she took for him an ark of bulrushes, and daubed it with slime and with pitch, and put the child therein, and laid it in the flags by the river's brink.

Once dressed, I place him in a basket woven tightly from reeds and cover him with a blue-and-white blanket, right up to his cleft chin, tucking it tightly all around. "It's all right," I coo as he fights to free himself and his round cheeks redden. "Don't struggle. Mama's here."

And the daughter of Pharaoh came down to bathe at the river; and her maidens walked along by the river's side.

I kneel, kiss his feverish forehead, and gently launch him into the river, where his woven cradle parts the water and floats slowly away, drifting achingly beyond my reach. His knit cap is the last thing I see before he falls below the horizon, his white cap indistinguishable from the other whitecaps cresting the waves.

And she saw the ark among the flags, and sent her handmaid to fetch it.

Celia. Celia will be there. She will find him on the other side.

And she opened it, and saw the child: and, behold, the babe wept.

Yes. Celia spreads her arms and casts her net upon the water. "Come, baby, come," she beckons, capturing him within the arc of powerful strokes that bring him ever closer, bobbing up and down, until he settles, coming to rest in the dark cleft between her breasts.

And she called his name Moses, and said, because I drew him out of the water.

No. His name is Rory. Call him Rory. He belongs to me.

CHAPTER FIFTEEN

Thursday
12:02 a.m.

My dream is broken by a distant yet insistent knocking. As I rise from the despairing depths of sleep, I realize that someone is at the door. I squint at Celia's alarm clock: 12:02 a.m. I've been asleep for less than an hour. *Edwina,* I think hopefully, *returning to see out the night by my side.*

Still dressed in a T-shirt and sweatpants, I stumble out of Celia's bed and open the door. I'm shocked to find not Edwina but Detective Constable Andrea Callaway, looking lank haired and tired, still wearing her oily trench coat and with a beige canvas messenger bag slung limply over her shoulder.

"DC Callaway," I croak. "Is something wrong?"

"Sorry to wake you, but you'll want to know—the body we pulled from the Thames this afternoon was not Cecelia Frost."

My mind, still foggy from sleep, struggles both to assemble a coherent thought and to maintain the secret that I've known for several hours. "Are you sure?" I ask, rubbing my eyes.

"Yes. May I come in?" Callaway angles her long torso through the doorway so I have no choice but to usher her inside.

"I'm sorry. Please do." I open the door and light from the hallway spills into the darkened flat, creeping across the threadbare carpet to single out the broken lamp, my riffled pile of clothing, the beige patina of flour still dusting the kitchenette floor.

As Callaway steps inside I close the door behind her and flip the light switch, bathing the flat in a harsh yellow glow. "I got your message that the place had been ransacked," she says, turning a full circle. "I expected worse."

"Edwina and I tried to clean up." I take Callaway's coat and drape it over the doorknob, then guide her to the kitchen table while I take the seat across from her. I have a feeling that her visit is about more than the identity of the dead body, and I steel myself for what is to come. "If it wasn't Celia you found, who was it?" I stare at the table, unable to make eye contact. Shakespeare said, *There is no art to find the mind's construction in the face*, but the fact that Celia is still alive, and I have seen her, feels visible, as if written on my skin.

Callaway folds her bony hands and rests them on the table. A tiny muscle twitches just above her lip. "Claire McAvoy. A twenty-three-year-old waitress."

"Oh." Celia is alive, but another woman isn't. And somewhere in London, a family grieves. "How did she die?" I ask softly.

"Strangled. Following a sexual assault."

I shudder. "That's awful."

Callaway's deep, rodent-like eyes dart around the flat, evaluating everything. Her gaze settles on the two used wineglasses still gracing the kitchen table. "I see you've had a visitor," she says evenly.

"That's right." She waits for me to say more, so I do. "Edwina."

She nods, raising her chin. "Indeed. And where is Edwina now?"

"At her flat, I'd imagine. Or maybe at her brother's." I look up suddenly. "Do you need to talk to her?"

"No. Well, yes," she corrects. "To inform her about the body, of course."

"Of course." I pause. "But that can probably wait until morning, don't you think?"

"I expect so."

A strained silence descends. In the absence of other sound, I can hear Callaway breathe and swallow. She holds me in her gaze, unblinking.

"DC Callaway, is there something else?" I finally ask. "Because if there isn't, I'd like to go back to bed. It's been a long day."

She sighs heavily, dropping her shoulders in a surprising release of pent-up tension that leaves her looking not just younger, but almost vulnerable. "It's late, so I'll level with you." She pauses. "I think you're hiding something."

"Hiding something? Like what?" I try to sound casual, but the break in my voice betrays me.

"I think you have information regarding the whereabouts of Cecelia Frost."

"What makes you say that?" My heart pounds and I feel my face redden. "Just because it wasn't Celia you found doesn't prove she's still alive."

"Perhaps not. But it seems less likely that she's dead."

"Look, if I knew where she was, why wouldn't I tell you? I want to find her as much as anybody does. I want to know if she's okay."

Callaway shifts in her seat, leans to one side, and reaches into her messenger bag. She pulls out a stack of photographs in a variety of shapes and sizes. "Have a look," she challenges, sliding the photos across the table.

"What are these?" I ask warily.

"Just take a look."

I shuffle through the pictures, which are horrific. They are police evidence photographs of victimized children, mostly girls but some boys too—bound, tortured, engaging in sex acts, with adults, with objects, with each other. The children's eyes and some facial features have been redacted, pixilated or blacked out to obscure their identities, but the terror can be read in their body language, in their rigid limbs and gaping mouths.

Before I make it through the entire pile, Callaway slaps another photo down in front of me, of a beautiful East Indian girl with soulful eyes, long black braided hair, and a dazzling smile, wearing gold necklaces and a colorful sari. "This is Asha. At age thirteen. Before her virginity was sold for one hundred and fifty pounds."

Callaway slaps down another photo. "This is what she looks like now."

My stomach twists as I push the picture away.

"Prepubescent girls are highly prized because they can be raped without using a condom," Callaway continues. "Those who refuse are mutilated and killed."

Another photo.

"This is Olga. From Moldova. She's seven years old. Lovely, isn't she? Or at least she used to be. The pedophiles insist Moldova has Europe's prettiest children."

Callaway's next photograph shows a group of scantily clad teenage girls rushing out the front door of a semidetached suburban home in what looks like a police raid, struggling to hide their faces and their naked breasts.

"These girls are older," she says softly. "Aged sixteen to nineteen. From Albania, Belarus, and Ukraine. Rescued last year from a house in Romford. But they can never go home. They have shamed their families and would likely end up back on the streets."

I close my eyes, not wanting to see more, but Callaway is relentless.

"Of course the victims aren't only Asian and European." She waits for me to open my eyes and look down. I do, then wish I hadn't.

"This child was purchased at a market in Abidjan, in the Ivory Coast, where little girls, their hair neatly braided and wearing their best Sunday dresses, can be purchased for as little as five to ten American dollars."

The next photo is a landscape scene featuring a rural dirt road lined by large convoy trucks and tin shacks with corrugated roofs. Picturesque mountain peaks are visible in the background.

I look up at Callaway, confused.

"This is Salgaa," she explains. "By day it's nothing but a dusty traffic stop on the Nakuru-Eldoret highway, the main road linking Kenya and Uganda. By night it's the world's biggest brothel, where hundreds of men pay as little as one or two pounds for sex. AIDS is rampant. Locals call the disease *mikingo*, meaning slow puncture, or *kauzi*, slim as a thread."

The next photo shows an African woman, naked and skeletal, lying on a narrow cot, her ashy skin slick with open sores and her hollow, unseeing eyes sunken deep into her bony skull. "This is Jelita. She is"—Callaway corrects herself—"she *was* nineteen." She pauses. "Her daughter has AIDS as well."

I can't bear it anymore. "Detective, what does any of this have to do with Celia?"

Callaway pauses before speaking. "We believe that Cecelia Frost has been working with a loosely organized Eastern European gang who traffic young women and girls into the UK and then around the world."

I shake my head. "You're wrong. Celia gets girls like these off the streets."

Callaway stiffens, squaring her shoulders. "She'd have you believe that."

"What do you mean?"

"She's created a reasonable cover," Callaway continues. "Apparently she rescues girls who are mentally deficient or too frail, ill, or damaged to be sold and finds them charity placements here in Britain. The stronger, healthier girls she helps groom for distribution. Then, once the girls are on their way, the mobsters give Celia a cut of their profits."

I force a hollow laugh. "Look around you, Detective. Does this look like the home of someone taking payoffs from the mob?"

Callaway gives the flat a cursory glance, then takes a deep breath before continuing. "No. But Cecelia may have set up an overseas bank account under a false name."

Marguerite Alderton. My stomach seizes. It can't be true.

"And she may also be funneling money into that account so as not to raise suspicion here."

When I don't respond, Callaway continues. "Perhaps she plans to leave the country and take up residence overseas under this assumed name."

Stunned, I say nothing.

"You didn't know she had an arrest record, did you?" Callaway asks gently.

I shake my head. "No. But those were only minor offenses," I add quickly. "Celia was never convicted of anything serious."

"Yes. She was."

"Of what?"

"Does it really matter, Dayle?" Callaway leans across the table, her breath hot against my cheek. "Aren't you at all curious as to what *else* she didn't tell you?"

I sit, speechless, trying to take it all in.

Reaching again into the messenger bag, Callaway removes two eight-by-ten-inch photos from a side pocket and passes them to me. "I hoped I wouldn't have to show you these."

Hand trembling, I look down at the first photo. It's a shadowy surveillance photo of Celia, in profile, standing across from two large, muscular, Slavic-looking men in black leather jackets, with a young blond woman cowering in the narrow space between them. The woman, early twenties, is thin and hunched, dressed in a tiny miniskirt and sheer nylon blouse with her arms crossed tightly across her chest, as if trying to hug away her fear.

Just behind the men and the woman is a white van with its back doors open, surrounded by what look like large, multicolored shipping containers. The photo might have been taken in the hold of a ferry, or in a large garage or storage unit.

In one man's clenched fist a small, rounded, light-colored object is visible. Celia reaches for the object.

The second photograph shows the same scene, only in close-up. The man's fist, now clearly visible, holds a roll of £50 notes, inches from Celia's waiting fingertips.

"This doesn't prove anything," I offer feebly.

Without saying a word, Callaway reaches into her canvas bag one more time, withdraws another photograph, and carefully places it on top of the stack of images in front of me.

I glance down at the photo and nearly gag. The picture shows three young women, dead, naked, and soaking wet, their bodies arranged side by side on a gravel beach beside a dark body of water. Their expressionless faces are creased and bloated, their hands bound and their feet encased in concrete. Their breasts have been hacked off, as if with a machete.

"This is what happens to those caught trying to escape their enslavement," Callaway says, her voice devoid of emotion. "It sends a message, keeps the other girls in line. The man responsible for this particular atrocity is Milan Gregorovich." She pauses. "He's the taller of the two men you see there in the photograph with Cecelia."

No. No. No. I turn the photograph over so only the white backside is visible, place it over the others, then slide the entire pile of photos back to Callaway.

Her thin, efficient fingers square the haphazard stack of photos so the edges line up. "Horrific, isn't it?"

"Yes," I manage to reply in a hoarse whisper.

"But this can be stopped, you know. It isn't hopeless."

"Isn't it?"

"The trafficking, I mean."

"Oh."

"Removing a single cog can significantly stall the machinery."

"Uh-huh." I close my eyes as my head begins to spin.

"A single cog. That's all we need."

"Yes." My arms and legs go weak.

"A single cog may not seem like much."

"No."

"But if we remove one cog here and another there, we can interrupt the flow." Callaway's voice is softer than I've ever heard it.

"I don't know…"

"But of course you do." She covers my hand with hers. "You know what's right."

Do I?

"I believe you *want* to tell me. It would be a relief."

"Celia," I whisper.

"What of Celia?"

"She's still alive."

"Go on."

"I saw her."

"When?"

"Around nine o'clock."

"Where?"

Outside, rain tickles the trees and taps faintly against the window.

"Where did you see her, Dayle?" Callaway's voice rises, but only slightly.

"At the London Eye."

"Is she still there?"

I shake my head. "No."

"Then where is she?"

"I don't know." My voice drops to a whisper. "But I'm supposed to meet her tomorrow."

"Where?" Callaway is nearly breathless.

If I tell the truth, there will be no turning back.

"At the Circle of Lebanon." I pause, swallowing hard. "Highgate Cemetery. Nine fifteen a.m."

Chapter Sixteen

Thursday
12:48 a.m.

"I'll make tea," Callaway offers as I slump at the kitchen table, trying to comprehend what I've just done. "Looks as if you could use some reviving."

I don't reply. Callaway strides into the kitchen and immediately goes to work, filling the electric kettle with cold water and searching the cupboards for tea bags and mugs. There is something prim and efficient in her gestures, in the straight-backed way she stands and the busy little noises she makes.

I rise and move to the window, then pull back the brocaded burgundy curtain, which, as I touch it, releases a thick mist of powder-gray dust that shimmies to the floor. I gaze out at the rain-slicked street and the row of tall brick town houses that rest, dark and quiet, with drapes drawn and shutters closed, as the towering oak and chestnut trees lining Rosslyn Hill seem to raise their arms and bow their heads, sheltering all that dwells beneath.

I glance over my shoulder at the clock on Celia's desk. It is nearing one a.m. If I go through with this, Celia has less than nine hours of freedom left.

Callaway squints at me from the kitchen. "Are you all right?" she asks. "You look rather pale."

I'm amazed she can gauge my complexion by the thin yellow light from the single bulb in the fixture above my head. "I'll be fine," I reply. "Once this is over."

"I understand. You must be gutted." She smiles sadly, tapping the handle of the kettle, and for one brief moment, she seems almost human. "There's nothing worse than being let down by a friend."

"I suppose not." I don't tell her how many worse things I am able to imagine.

She turns back to the kettle, testing the warmth with her palm. I try to imagine Callaway in a different environment—at home, or perhaps at the police station just up the road. I picture her in an office on the second floor, where the fluorescent lights are buzzing and the desks are manned by plainclothes detectives and bleary-eyed Metropolitan Police officers in uniform typing up reports on blinking computer screens. Callaway's desk, messy yet impersonal, will offer nothing more revealing than a crushed pack of Lambert & Butler cigarettes, a chain of linked paper clips, a ball of rubber bands, and a torn wrapper from a Bounty bar, its ragged edges sealed with a dried chocolate thumbprint. There will be no photos, knickknacks, or hastily scribbled grocery lists, not even an orphaned earring that might provide a glimpse of the real DC Andrea Callaway hidden beneath the greasy hair and soiled trench coat.

The tea made, Callaway brings the mugs to the table and gestures for me to join her. I take a seat and stare down at the thin brownish-gray liquid swirling inside the chipped ceramic mug.

"Sorry it's not stronger," she apologizes. "I used what was left of the milk."

"That's okay. It's one a.m. I don't need the caffeine."

She reaches into her messenger bag and pulls out a notepad and pen. "Still trying to take it all in, I'd imagine."

"You could say that."

She pulls her chair closer to the table and leans heavily on her elbows. "You're doing her a favor, you know."

"How's that?"

"If Cecelia stays in London, the mobsters will kill her. They have already threatened her—they would have no qualms about taking her life. Attacking her in the street and stealing her handbag is nothing, compared to what they might do." She uncaps her pen. "And if Cecelia tries to leave the UK, she will be arrested. If not by me or my team, then by other authorities who may not be so"—she pauses—"generous."

"Generous?"

She nods solemnly. "Yes. We can offer Cecelia a deal that will spare her serving any jail time."

Callaway has not, so far, appeared to be the conciliatory type. "Why would you do that?"

"Because Cecelia Frost is a small fish." She frowns, scribbling on her pad in an attempt to bring forth ink. "There's no currency in prosecuting her. We are targeting the ringleaders behind this whole operation. We can never completely stop the trafficking of young women into Britain, but we can curtail the trade, at least temporarily, by bringing down a few key players."

I sip my tea. "And you need Celia's help."

Callaway nods. "Celia knows these people as well as anyone. Her information would be invaluable."

I put down the mug. "The minute she snitches on these guys, her life will be worthless. She might just as well jump into the Thames."

"Oh, we don't want her to grass." Callaway pauses. "We want her to testify."

"Testify?"

"In court. And in exchange, we'll guarantee her protection for life."

"You can do that?"

"Yes. She'll get a new name and identity, a home of her own, money, support, whatever she needs. Most importantly, we'll see that she is protected. Permanently."

Exactly what Celia was trying to create for herself in the US. But this way, she'll have plenty of help. And the British taxpayer foots the bill.

Callaway flips her notepad to the next clean sheet. "Let's review the details of your plan to meet."

"There's not much to tell." I sip the lukewarm tea, which grows more bitter as it cools. "We are supposed to meet at the tomb of Radclyffe Hall. The Circle of Lebanon, Highgate Cemetery. Nine fifteen a.m."

Her eyebrows rise as she taps the notepad. "Why there? Why then?"

I shrug. "It was Celia's suggestion. Radclyffe Hall's *The Well of Loneliness* is her favorite novel so the spot has special significance. There's a red duffel bag in the wardrobe. I'm supposed to bring that with me, filled with her clothes, a cell phone, and cash, and give it to her outside the tomb."

Callaway nods, trying to seem casual, but her deep beady eyes are on fire. "I see. Then what's meant to happen?"

"Go our separate ways, I suppose."

"Do you know her specific travel details?"

I could say no. Or I could lie and say something completely outlandish. There is still time to save Celia, if I so choose. But is Celia still worth saving? The Celia I knew—or the Celia I *thought* I knew?

I take a deep breath. "Celia plans to take the ten past five train from Euston to Holyhead and then sail to Dublin."

"Will she be traveling alone?"

"I believe so."

"And will she be traveling under an assumed name?"

Don't tell—don't tell—don't tell—the words pound through my skull. "Marguerite Alderton," I reply softly.

The wheels are turning as Callaway licks her thin lips. "All right then," she pronounces, "we'll follow you to Highgate. Once you hand over the gym bag, we will arrest her."

Instantly the scene plays out in my imagination—the look of absolute horror on Celia's face as she realizes that I have betrayed her. *You want me to be Judas. And mark her with my kiss.*

"Isn't there some other way?" I ask, panicking.

"What do you mean?"

"Can't you arrest her later?"

She frowns. "Later?"

"After we leave the cemetery. Can't you arrest her at Euston?"

"Does it matter where we arrest her?"

"Yes. I don't want her to know."

"Know what?"

"That I turned her in."

Callaway shakes her head. "We can't afford to wait. Once we locate her, we need to act quickly."

My mind races. No. There has to be another way. "Can't you follow her from the cemetery after I give her the duffel bag? She'll be at Euston—she has nowhere else to go."

"I'm sorry." Callaway coldly pats my hand. Having gotten what she needs, she's reverted to official-police-business mode. "Cecelia might change her plans. Or she may not have told you the truth. We can't take the chance she'll slip away." Callaway forces a smile, but her eyes remain deadly still. "For her own protection, of course. Her life is still in danger. We can keep her safe."

"DC Callaway." I form the words carefully. "I didn't have to tell you where she is, or even agree to help you. I think you owe me something in return."

A muscle above Callaway's lip twitches, even as she refuses to blink.

"Don't make me watch as you arrest her." My voice breaks. "Imagine if she were your best friend."

Callaway scowls at her notes and I go in for the kill.

"This won't work if you and I don't trust each other." Her eyes flicker and I know she's mine. "Please. Don't make me beg."

"Very well. I'm not thrilled, mind you. But we do appreciate your assistance." Frowning, she quickly pages through her notes. "All right, here is what we will do. You will meet Miss Frost at the tomb of Radclyffe Hall at a quarter past nine. You will hand over the bag she is expecting, with the items inside. The two of you will leave the cemetery together and then separate. One of my men will arrest Cecelia later, at Euston Station."

By the look on Callaway's narrow face I suspect she is lying. *You are going to arrest Celia the moment we leave the cemetery. If not before.* But now it's too late. I've said too much.

Callaway glances at her watch. "If you'd like to come back to the station, we've got a quiet room with a settee, a pillow, and some blankets. You can get a few hours' rest before your rendezvous."

"Thanks, but I'd rather stay here."

"Are you certain?" She eyes me suspiciously.

"Yes. I'm certain."

Callaway is about to say more when her cell phone rings. She reaches into her coat pocket, withdraws the phone, and pops it open in a single gesture.

"DC Callaway. What? No, I was just leaving. I hadn't heard." She holds the phone away from her face and covers it with her hand, anxiously leaning across the table.

"What is it?" I ask.

"Police in Birmingham have arrested seven members of a terrorist cell preparing to attack London." Her voice bristles with excitement. "They've caught the ringleader as well as the would-be bombers. The threat is over! They've been caught."

CHAPTER SEVENTEEN

Thursday
1:31 a.m.

I turn on the television and click through the channels but the story is so fresh it hasn't yet reached the media. From her colleague, Callaway gleans that the Birmingham terrorist cell was composed of homegrown hard-core fundamentalists, all born and raised in England, and that the tip that broke the whole case open came via a phone call from a member of the public, who reported that her neighbor's son was behaving "strangely."

"It's extraordinary," Callaway remarks, snapping closed her cell phone and shaking her head. "Young men willing to betray their own nation. Treachery at the deepest level."

As she speaks, I understand that not only is true treachery silent and interior, it can take many forms. "How could these young men do it?" I ask rhetorically. "And yet, some will question the woman who turned in her neighbor's son."

"*That* was an act of courage," Callaway insists, eyes flashing.

"I agree," I reply. "But there will be some who see it as an act of betrayal. It's all in how you look at things, I believe."

❖

After we review the Highgate plan one final time, Callaway prepares to leave. I escort her downstairs, bidding good-bye at the front door. Then I quickly make my way back up the split staircase and enter Celia's flat for what I know will be the final time. Celia, too, will never again set foot inside this cramped and dreary little room that has been her home for more than two years. The whole life that was lived here—the relief center she founded and ran, the books and articles she wrote, the body that moved through this space, the heart that felt the loss of a father, everything she thought and hoped and dreamed and cared about—all about to be dismantled. A life can seem so small, and never smaller than in its unraveling.

But now is not the time to be sentimental, not when I only have a few hours until I meet again with Celia. I know what Callaway said; the photos she showed me were overwhelming, but I have to be certain. I have to find out from Celia if what the police accuse her of is true. In the back of my mind, I suspect it might be. But I have to be sure.

I change clothes and pack quickly, filling my suitcase, my laptop bag, and my backpack, along with the red duffel bag from inside Celia's wardrobe, which I stuff with Celia's clean clothes, the cell phone, credit card, and £5000 cash. It has to look right. In case I *do* let them arrest her.

I grab whatever other useful items I can scavenge from the flat, which isn't much—scissors, Kleenex, a bar of soap, a couple of pens, and the box of black hair dye. I scour the kitchen for anything potentially edible but find only a can of Foster's beer, a small plastic-wrapped meat pie, and a Lyle's Golden Syrup cake.

I phone for a taxi and can just about handle the luggage with the backpack on my back, the laptop bag over one shoulder, and the duffel bag over the other, while I pull the suitcase with my one good hand. As I step into the hallway, the door to the flat slams closed behind me, rattling my bones like a stone rolled over the entrance to a tomb.

Once I maneuver myself and the luggage downstairs and out the front door, I find the cab waiting for me, parked at a provocative angle and with impatient puffs of exhaust belching from its tailpipe.

I am hurrying toward the curb when a timid voice behind me suddenly calls out, "Excuse me, miss?" I spin so quickly I nearly trip over my luggage. As I straighten, a tipsy figure teeter-totters out of the shadows and into the light. "They tell me you can help."

It is a girl, maybe fifteen, with long, straight dark hair parted down the middle, and dressed in a tiny denim miniskirt, bright red stilettos, and a too-tight white knit cardigan over a sheer yellow blouse open nearly to her waist. She must be freezing out here.

"I'm sorry," I say quickly, "my cab…"

She toddles closer, nearly twisting her ankle. "Please, miss. I can't go back." Her voice, Irish accented, quivers as she tries to be brave. "They say this place is safe. And that Cecelia Frost can help."

I set down the duffel bag and glance at my cab waiting across the street, worried he'll leave and I'll lose precious time phoning for another. "What's your name, child?" I ask with a sigh.

My question seems to surprise her. "N-Niamh," she sputters, and I know her name is definitely not Niamh. Mary or Margaret or Sinead—anything but Niamh. As she takes another step, I see the bruises along her jaw and red splotches decorating her neck. Her blouse is not open but torn, nearly in two. She only just got away. Next time she might not be so lucky.

"Niamh, Cecelia Frost isn't here. But I know someone who can help." Struggling to open my backpack with one hand, I slip Niamh three £20 notes and the business card that Sophie Jameson had given me at the hospital, then point to the cab across the street. "That cab is waiting. Tell him you're going to Hope House. The address is on the card. When you get there, ask for Sophie Jameson. She'll help you out."

Niamh stuffs the money into her back pocket and considers the card, tipping it toward the streetlight and squinting suspiciously. She opens her mouth to speak but I cut her off.

"Go on. Get out of here. Before I change my mind," I say brusquely. She nods in understanding and pockets the card, then bends, steps out of her stilettos, and runs delicately barefoot across the street, clutching the sharply angled shoes that bounce rapidly against her hip.

Whoever or whatever else Celia may be, she will never be any less than a hero to the people she helped, I think bleakly. I take out my cell phone but before I even punch the first number, a black cab turns the corner onto Rosslyn Hill and I hail him furiously, waving my good arm like a flag.

"So glad I caught you," I say as I open the door and pile the luggage into the backseat with no help from him, despite the cast on my arm. I glance into the front seat and see the meter ticking quickly. I've already wasted too much time.

"Where may I transport you, miss?" the cabbie asks as I struggle to close the door. I look up and see that he is young and handsome, possessing a cruel beauty made up of slim lips, smooth skin, and very round dark eyes. His cab is spotless and he is dressed surprisingly formally in a dress shirt and tie. I imagine he is Somali or Sudanese, some type of North African.

"Bayswater," I reply.

"Bayswater. Yes, miss. Where, precisely?"

"I'm not exactly sure. I'll let you know when we get there."

He nods solemnly. "As you wish, madame."

There is little traffic this time of night so it doesn't take long to reach Bayswater, a tacky-touristy area jam-packed with Indian takeaways and fast-food joints, souvenir shops, youth hostels, and cheap bed-and-breakfasts. It's the perfect place to blend in, to hide from Callaway and the police's prying eyes. A place where I can confront Celia and find out the truth.

I have the driver take me up and down the numerous side streets off the main thoroughfare. The streets, nearly deserted at this hour save for a few homeless people and a handful of stumbling drunks, are lined with deceptively elegant-looking town houses, three or four stories high, featuring cream-colored brick, wrought-iron railings, and tall, porticoed columns. Upon closer inspection, though, these seemingly grand buildings are in fact ramshackle and unkempt, with peeling paint, cracked windows, and signs advertising *Full English Breakfast* and *Double Rm £100 Nt.*

As we drive I can't help but think about the girl, Niamh-whose-name-is-not-Niamh, wondering if she's reached Hope House yet, if Sophie Jameson is this very moment showing her the army cot where she will sleep, and handing her a scratchy hand towel and a brand-new, unwrapped bar of soap that Niamh will clutch like a rosary, pressing it to her face and inhaling deeply the fresh clean scent of lavender.

Even if Niamh is safe, there are so many like her still out here, lurking in the shadows, ducking into corners, huddled at bus stops, frightened and alone. An army of missing girls, invisible women, and discarded, throwaway children. More than anything I want to know that my son is all right. Gone, perhaps, but not lost; bundled up somewhere, in a place beyond my reach. Safe and at peace, cradled in the arms of a great someone.

I have the driver stop in front of the Greenland House Hotel, a white three-story town house that displays both a Union Jack and an Australian flag in its front window. It's a modest-looking establishment, the second from the end in a row of run-down lodgings. I ask the driver to wait while I check to see if I can book a room for the night. He nods solemnly, half closing his eyes.

The only available room is located in the damp, foul-smelling basement, where the floor is concrete and the scant light comes from a bare bulb swinging on a chain overhead. The room itself, cramped and dingy, has just one double bed. At least the bathroom, although filthy and ringed with mold, is en suite. I tell the desk clerk I'll take the room: one night, two guests. I have no choice—I'm running out of time and I have to find Celia.

I deposit my luggage in the room, struggle to close and lock the warped wooden door, then return to the waiting cab with nothing but my backpack over my shoulder.

"Now to Gospel Oak," I say, breathless from rushing up the stairs. "Gospel Oak Primary School, to be precise."

Suddenly the driver seems more interested and his dark eyes widen. "Do you seek a companion for the evening?" he asks.

"You could say that," I reply, settling back as he peels away from the curb.

I don't have time to chase all over London looking for Celia, so I have to stake everything on my belief that Gospel Oak Primary School is where she would spend what she believes to be her final night in England. When we shared our flat in Clapham, Celia would often spend a full Sunday afternoon at the primary school, sitting on the playground swings and brooding. The place had a special resonance for her because it was within sight of where her mother had died. When Celia was a toddler, Maggie, then age forty-two and suffering from terminal brain cancer, threw herself in front of a train at the Gospel Oak station, just a few minutes' walk from the school and playground.

Celia made this regular pilgrimage not to feel close to her mother, the dead being for Celia only and always dead, but to contemplate Maggie's final act while imagining the last things her mother saw, heard, and felt before she died. For Celia this became a way of facing the loss and abandonment, by staring, unblinking, into the abyss of her own grief.

The school is located on Mansfield Road, a quiet residential street near the southeastern corner of Hampstead Heath. The school itself is a nondescript 1970s-looking two-story building, long and narrow, with a flat roof and rows of small square windows. I have the driver wait in front of the school, promising I'll be back in twenty or thirty minutes. When he looks skeptical, I give him a £50 note, a deposit for the £78 I owe him so far.

The large, modern playground is in the back, behind the school buildings, and well appointed with basketball hoops, soccer nets, and monkey bars. The grounds, as I enter, appear to be deserted, and I am struck by the hushed, eerie, otherworldly quality that a child's play area can take on at night. It is as if under cover of darkness the ghosts of children long since gone rise up again to mingle and dance, while the echo of their lost laughter moves across an invisible threshold, parting the damp blades of grass as it passes.

Celia is not where I expect to find her, on the canvas swings opposite the red metal slide. But in the distance, on the playground's periphery, I see a lone figure, smoking, huddled at the end of a wooden bench, illuminated by a muted pool of sulfur-colored light spilling from a streetlamp overhead. Blue-gray plumes of smoke emerge from the figure's mouth in a steady rhythm, in and out, briefly circling the head like a ghostly garland before retreating, dissolving into the blankness of night. Celia. It has to be.

I approach, walking quickly, and as I draw closer she looks up with a start. When I am within thirty feet she withdraws a knife from the pocket of her denim jacket, the glint of the silver blade catching and reflecting the light. When she realizes it is me, she smiles, her small teeth flashing brightly in the dark.

"We weren't supposed to meet until quarter past nine," she calls out, sliding the knife back into her pocket.

"I couldn't wait that long," I reply.

"How did you know I'd be here?" She squints behind her cigarette, shivering from the cold.

"A lucky guess?"

"Right." She scoots over and I sit down on the bench beside her with my right side pressed against her left. For a moment I revel in the familiar feel of her thin body, brittled by exhaustion, and absorb the full force of a life that a few hours ago I was certain no longer existed. All my fears, questions, and doubts disappear and this is Cecelia Frost, my Celia, the Celia I've known since I was thirteen. She couldn't be guilty of the terrible things Callaway claimed. So why don't I just *ask* her?

"You're freezing." I put my arm around her shoulders and rub her sinewy bicep. Her clothing is damp and she shivers. "You aren't dressed for this weather. Were you planning to stay here all night?"

"No, but for as long as I could manage it," she admits, dropping her chin to her chest and withdrawing for warmth. "I try never to stay in one place more than a few hours. I'm still not certain who may be following me."

She offers me her nearly finished cigarette but I decline, shaking my head. She shrugs, takes a final puff, then tosses it to the ground and stubs it out. We are both quiet for several moments, listening intently to the muffled dark, waiting for shape or sound to emerge and assert itself. "This place has changed greatly," Celia finally says, surveying the school and the playground. "Back in the seventies and eighties, they had little prefabs scattered about back here, to handle the overflow of students."

I try to visualize the scene. "That must have looked weird," I offer.

"Indeed." She blows on her palms, then rubs her hands for warmth. "This place was bombed during the war, you know."

"Really? The Germans bombed a grade school?"

Celia nods. "Yes. Although it is believed that the Luftwaffe were actually aiming for the railway station and hit the school by mistake."

"Oh." I stare out at the multicolored circles, squares, and other shapes that divide up the playground's smooth black surface, delineations for games I will probably never witness or understand. "I've always loved the history here," I whisper. "London. The UK. Europe. It's as if every inch of space contains several generations of stories."

"Yes. And my own history is here too," Celia adds softly. "Mum died just over the road." She gestures with the shrug of one shoulder, not bothering to turn around.

I nod. "Yes, I remember you telling me. Gospel Oak railway station."

Celia spreads her fingers, indicating the width of the playground, from the school buildings to the street. "And this is where they found me."

"They found you?" I ask, confused.

She nods. "I was here."

"What do you mean?" My skin prickles. "You were *here* when she died?"

"Yes. I was here on the playground while Mum was busy, off killing herself."

CHAPTER EIGHTEEN

Thursday
3:51 a.m.

I shudder at the image of the toddler Celia, orphaned on the swings, waiting hopefully for the mother who will never return.

"I think, originally, she intended for me to die too." Celia shivers, plunging her hands into her pockets. "I believe she planned to throw herself in front of the train with me in her arms. But something changed her mind."

In my head an already bleak scene grows steadily darker and I feel the need to defend a long-dead woman I never met. "Your mother was terminally ill," I propose. "Maybe she thought she couldn't bear to leave you behind. But when she got here, she felt differently."

Celia bristles. "My mother was not sentimental."

"But I am?"

"No. You're not sentimental, you're just"—she lowers her voice—"*American*." She pauses. "You know what I mean."

Ignoring the insult, I continue. "I believe your mother wanted you to live. That's what any woman would hope for, that her child might survive and go on without her."

Celia pokes a pebble with her toe, coaxing it to turn over. "I remember I was wearing my favorite coat, white wool with a fur collar. Mum sat me on the swing with an ice cream, then shoved a scrap of paper in my pocket. As she walked away, she turned and waved. When I waved back, I dropped my ice cream and started to cry. I looked up and she was gone."

Celia shakes her head. "There must have been a great commotion at the station, but I heard nothing. They found me an hour later, still waiting. Inside my pocket was the scrap of paper with my name, my father's name, our address, and phone number." Celia's voice is soft but steady, devoid of emotion.

"I found the little white coat neatly folded in a box beneath the bed when I cleared out Dad's things after he died. So unlike him to keep it all these years. The scrap of paper was still in the pocket—someone must have shoved it back in there after ringing Dad."

Celia has moved on, but I haven't; I remain with the lonely little girl on the swing set, grieving an ice-cream cone and not yet aware of the great loss to come.

"So you see, Dayle, I've deceived you," Celia suddenly confesses.

Is this it? Is she about to tell me everything? "Deceived me?" My heart races as I struggle to keep my voice steady. "In what way?"

Celia drops her chin. "I never came here to imagine what my mother had seen. I came to remember what *I* had seen, all those years ago. I've often felt there was something more, something I knew then but have since forgotten." She flips the pebble with her foot, then grinds her heel into the dampened soil.

"You didn't have to keep that a secret." I hunch my shoulders against the wind as I realize her revelation is a false alarm. "I would have understood."

She shrugs. "I suppose it's not important, in the grand scheme of things."

"No, I'm your friend. I should have known," I argue. "We can never understand another person's heart, can we?"

"No. We humans are unfathomable." She gives a sly smile that narrows her eyes. "We barely even know ourselves."

"Come on, let's go." I rise wearily from the bench.

She frowns. "We can't return to my flat."

"I know. I got us a room."

"Where?"

"Bayswater. Not exactly five star, but it'll do for tonight." I hesitate. "Are you still planning to take the ten past five to Holyhead?"

"Yes."

"Good. You can get a decent night's sleep before you leave."

"Cheers, Dayle." Her smile is genuine as she too rises from the wooden bench and turns away from the wind. "I owe you, my friend."

We return to the street, where my taxi waits in front of the school. If Celia is not what the driver expected of my midnight rendezvous, he doesn't say a word. "Back to the B and B, please," I tell him as Celia and I climb into the backseat.

My head is still reeling as Celia leans back and closes her eyes. The moment I close my own eyes, I see only the photographs Callaway showed me earlier. How can I reconcile those horrific images with the Celia sitting beside me, so close I can feel her breathing? Suddenly Celia stirs and squints out the foggy window.

"We're like spies, you and me," she says in a tone that's unreadable.

"What do you mean?"

"All this. Me using a false name to evade Russian mobsters." She laughs bleakly. "And you—Miss American Pie, so sweet and wholesome, good Wisconsin girl."

"What about me?"

Celia's face flashes from darkness to light as the cab sails beneath streetlamps. "Here you are, whisked into a van by stone-faced Samoans and deposited at the London Eye, clandestine meetings on a deserted playground, late-night rendezvous at a cheap B and B. You aren't Dayle Salvesen. Hell, you aren't even Candee Cronin. You know who you are?"

"I'm sure you'll tell me."

"Redleigh Smith. The *real* Redleigh Smith." She winks. "Turns out your books are actually autobiographical."

"Right."

"No, I'm serious. All you need is the bulletproof Kevlar bra. And the stiletto heel that doubles as a switchblade."

"Don't forget the tampon that transforms into a personal floatation device in the event of a water landing." I smile, in spite of everything. "But if I'm Redleigh Smith, then I have those things already."

"True." Celia folds her narrow arms and shakes her head. "We've come a long way from the two prepubescent girls writing a musical stage version of *Gulliver's Travels*."

Instantly I remember—the drafty junior-high lunchroom, the greasy pizza and rock-hard Tater Tots on plastic trays hastily pushed aside to make room for the masterpiece we scribbled into our ring binders and notebooks.

"Tragically bookish, we were." Celia sighs. "Were we always in the lunch room or holed up in some dusty library?"

"We knew how to have fun," I argue.

"We made our own fun," she corrects. "Thick as thieves, Dad used to say." Suddenly her face darkens and she shifts toward the window. We've reached St. John's Wood, a wealthy residential area of luxury apartments and gated, multi-million-dollar homes, and just passed Lord's Cricket Ground, a sprawling sports field that is cricket's equivalent to Yankee Stadium. "Excuse me, why did you turn there?" Celia demands of the driver. "You should have taken Edgware Road."

The driver ignores her.

"Listen—cut back over to Edgware Road, please." Celia's voice is taut, angry. "Now. I insist."

"Lisson Grove, miss," the driver mumbles.

"What?" Celia shakes the back of the driver's seat.

"Lisson Grove," I repeat. "This will get us to Bayswater the same as Edgware." I try to sound casual, but I'm scared. I glance over my shoulder to see if we're being followed. We aren't.

Celia says something to the driver in angry-sounding Arabic. He shoots back an angrier reply.

I start to speak, but Celia silences me with a quick scowl and shake of her head. She makes another, quieter comment in Arabic and sits back in her seat. Then she reaches into her pocket for her knife. I'm terrified of what she might do. With her right hand she grasps the door handle while with her left she coolly caresses the half-exposed knife, testing the blade against her fingertip. She nods for me to be ready to flee, should the need arise. We are silent the rest of the way as our unspoken fear rides between us, an unwelcome passenger taking up too much space.

She is hardened, I think to myself. This life has hardened her. The truth is, I have no idea what she's capable of.

❖

Celia's fears prove to be unfounded as we reach the Bayswater bed-and-breakfast without further incident. Feeling guilty I tip the driver an extra £30, but his elegant, shadowy face is inscrutable as he pockets the money and speeds away.

Celia and I trudge up the steps and into the B and B, where our after-hours arrival elicits barely a grunt in greeting from the hirsute and surly clerk, leaning back in his chair reading *The Sun* with his bare, hairy feet crossed atop the check-in desk. Celia glances around the damp, drab lobby, then peers into the darkened breakfast room where thimble-size juice glasses are stacked upside down on the sideboard, next to a wicker basket of plastic cutlery and a toaster from 1983. With a stab of embarrassment I wish I had found someplace nicer for us to spend the night.

We make our way down the creaky, uncarpeted staircase to the basement, illuminated by the single bulb swinging overhead, throwing just enough light to reveal the lines of damp rising tidally up the walls. I take the key from my pocket and unlock the warped wooden door to our room, struggling to push it free from its ill-fitting frame. Celia joins the effort, ramming the door with her shoulder. Finally the door lets loose and we stumble into the room, righting ourselves just past the transom.

I flip the light switch and notice, with despair, that the room's décor seems to have deteriorated while I was away and the space no longer appears fit for human habitation. My eyes dart in horror from the thin beige bedspread, stained and cigarette burned, to the high, narrow window caged by rusty metal bars flaking away in shades of orange and fiery brown, to the thin black crack in the fingerprinted mirror hung crookedly above the chest of drawers. The entire room is permeated with the odor of sweat, stale beer, and spoiled tandoori.

"I'm sorry, Celia," I say, unzipping my jacket. "I know it's awful."

"Aw, it's not so bad." She shrugs. "Better than a park bench, anyway. I'm desperate for a hot shower and a lie-down."

"That will have to wait." I take off my jacket and place it on the bed.

"Wait for what?"

"We have to talk. It's important."

"All right." If she's worried about what I'm going to say, she doesn't show it. "But first, I'm dying for the loo." She strides to the bathroom and pees lazily, not bothering to close the door. My heart races while I wait.

"Right." She returns moments later to sit on the edge of the bed, crossing one leg beneath her and sliding off her sweaty boots. "Now what is so bloody important?" She scratches her big toe with a fingernail.

I turn the chair so it's facing Celia and sit down, cradling my cast. "The police know we're meeting at the cemetery."

Her head shoots up and she is instantly on edge. "How could they?"

"I told them."

"You *told* them? Why?"

I take a deep breath. "There's a detective, Andrea Callaway, who claims you work with Eastern European gangsters trafficking young women, and that you profit from this relationship financially."

Celia pales with fury, throwing her blackened eye and fading facial scar into high relief. "And you *believed* that?"

"No." I shake my head. "Not at first. But then she showed me some photos…"

"Photos?"

"Of women. Children. Victims. They were horrible."

"Dayle, I would never do anything—"

"And you were in one of the pictures."

Her fury turns to shock. "Me?"

"Yes. It was a surveillance photograph of you with a man named Milan Gregorovich. Do you know him?"

She nods, blinking rapidly. "Of course. He's one of the ringleaders. But I never—"

"Met him? Celia, in the picture he was paying you."

"Paying me?"

"Yes. There was a close-up photo of your hand, accepting money."

Celia bows her head and clutches her face. She breathes quickly and for a moment I think she is weeping. "What else was in the photo?" she finally whispers, peering dry eyed from between her slim fingers.

"Another man, Slavic looking, next to Gregorovich." The photo is so seared into my memory I can still see every detail. "And between them, a woman. Early twenties, thin, blond, in a short skirt and sheer blouse, looking terrified."

Celia's words emerge slowly, softened by her hands. "Could you see shipping containers, as if the picture had been taken in the hold of a ferry?"

How does she know this? "Yes."

Celia looks up and her solemn face is spotted where her fingers pressed the skin. "Dayle, Gregorovich wasn't paying me. I was paying him."

"For what?"

"Anastasia. The woman in the photo. Her older sister had been trafficked into Britain six months earlier. Anastasia was working as a prostitute in Kiev when Gregorovich took possession of her. She had TB, so Sophie Jameson offered her placement at Hope House and medical treatment if I got her to London. So I paid Gregorovich at Dover to turn her over to me."

My head spins and it's my turn to be shocked. "You mean you bought another human being?"

"In a word, yes." Celia catches my reaction and her anger flares. "Don't be so naïve, Dayle. This is how the real world works. It's not pleasant and it's not pretty, but it's the truth. Anastasia was ill. Her earning potential was limited, so Gregorovich let her go. For a price, of course." She bites the words off bitterly. "If you don't believe me, ask Sophie. Because you can't ask Anastasia. She died three months ago. Caught pneumonia and deteriorated very quickly, I'm afraid."

Oh no. What have I done? To say I'm sorry, seems, at the moment anyway, completely inappropriate. So instead I stare down at the swollen, mottled fingers of my plaster-cast hand. We are both silent, listening to the stumbling lovers and broken bottles rolling through the street above our window. Occasionally a car passes, casting drab patterns on the wall and leaving in its wake the echo of a lonely engine whine.

"So what was the plan, exactly, for our meeting at the cemetery?" Celia's eyes are hooded, her voice flat and defeated. "And you had better tell me everything."

I take a deep breath and rise from the chair, stalking the tiny room's perimeter, avoiding my jagged reflection in the fractured mirror. "We meet at the tomb of Radclyffe Hall at nine fifteen. I hand you the duffel bag with the travel items. We separate. The police arrest you at Euston Station this evening, as you board the train to Holyhead."

Celia delves a nervous hand through her brittle hair, strafing her scalp. "Why not arrest me at the cemetery?"

"I asked them not to."

She looks confused.

"I didn't want you to know that I was the one who turned you in."

Her hazel eyes flash. "You didn't think I'd suss it out eventually?"

"I don't know. I suppose so," I admit. "I just didn't want to see your face when you realized it was me. Celia, Callaway made it sound so good! She said that if you testified against the Russians, the police would put you in a kind of witness protection program, give you a new identity, money, a home, a chance to start over, with lots of support. That's why I agreed to help them. I thought you'd be better off, in the long run."

"Well, thanks for your concern." Celia throws herself back on the mattress, knees bent and fingers laced behind her head. "What the hell am I going to do?"

My mind races, searching for a way to make this right. If I got her into this mess, I can get her out. "It's still the middle of the night," I offer hopefully. "You have time to get away. I'll go to the cemetery at nine fifteen, as if for the meeting, but you don't show up. If the police are there, I'll stall them. Send them off on a wild-goose chase. Meanwhile you take the Eurostar to Paris or something. Just get out of England and we'll connect once you're free. I'll help you get to America."

Celia jumps off the bed and paces, assaulting the stained carpet with her stocking feet. "Does Callaway know I'm traveling as Marguerite Alderton?"

For a moment I'm not certain, then I remember. "Yes." My stomach clenches. "I told her."

Celia shakes her head vigorously. "Then it won't work. It's unlikely I'll be out of England by quarter past nine, and if I don't show up at the cemetery, the police might check airports, ferries, the Channel Tunnel."

"But if you are innocent, why does it matter?" I step toward the bathroom. "Once you explain about Gregorovich, they'll let you go."

"Not necessarily. I can't be sure what the police know, or think they know, about my activities."

I stop dead in my tracks. "What activities?"

"Activities," she snaps. "It's too complicated to explain. But the police may try to charge me with a crime. I have no way of knowing what kind of false evidence they may have. And then I might never get out of England."

"So what are we going to do?"

Celia sinks to the bed and draws her knees to her chest, wrapping her arms around her narrow shins and holding them tightly. I step into the bathroom, where I cannot avoid my pale, guilty face in the mirror. I fill a glass with water and take it to Celia.

"There's only one option." She gulps down the water and then nervously rolls the glass between her palms.

"What's that?"

"Turn myself in."

"What do you mean?"

"In the morning we go to the nearest police station and I throw myself on their mercy. I'll testify against the traffickers and assume a new identity. Dayle, I never took payoffs from Gregorovich. But I am guilty of enough other things." She puts down the glass and rests her chin on her kneecap, seeming resigned. "The truth is, I've been playing a very dangerous game for some time now. It was bound to catch up with me eventually. Maybe it's time to move on." Her face, as she smiles, looks almost serene as some residual English spirit rises to the surface. Her people survived the Germans, after all. Even when the Luftwaffe bombed their schools.

"Are you sure? Because I will help you leave England tonight, if you like."

"I'll be fine, Dayle." Celia purses her lips and forces a determined grin. "This could be the fresh start I was looking for. Only here in the UK, rather than the States."

"But you realize, if you testify against the Russians and go into witness protection, we will never see each other ever again," I remind her.

She lifts one shoulder and smiles sadly. "Then I suppose we must make the best of the little time we have left."

CHAPTER NINETEEN

Thursday
4:43 a.m.

Suddenly Celia jumps off the bed and roots through the duffel bag, tossing aside clothing, scissors, a ballpoint pen. She pulls out the box of black hair dye and holds it up over her shoulder. "Why bring this?" she asks.

"I don't know." I grab my backpack and attempt to unzip it with my good hand.

"Let me guess—you hadn't yet decided if you were going to help me leave England or turn me in to the police."

Unable to look her in the eye, I search the backpack for my T-shirt and sweats. "Celia, what do you want me to say?"

"Dayle, did you really imagine I was guilty?" Her voice is soft as she slices open the box of dye with her fingernail. "That I could take money by exploiting innocent women and children?"

I plop down on the bed and pull the backpack into my lap. "I didn't want to believe Callaway," I explain. "But I was exhausted, scared, confused. I just wanted her to leave me alone."

"Do you believe me now?"

"Yes. I do."

She squeezes the box and grins mischievously. "Then help me cut my hair and dye it black."

"Why? I'm sure they'll give you a makeover in witness protection."

"I know. But this way I'll look more like you."

A series of police sirens wails past our window. I wait until they pass before I speak. "Why would you want to look like me?"

"So when we're parted, I'll still see your face when I look in the mirror."

She must catch my shocked reaction because she turns away, sets down the box, and peels off her grubby white T-shirt. "Bollocks," she mutters, shaking her head. "I've gone soft. If you tell anyone I said that, I'll have you done. I have some *highly* dangerous associates, as you well know."

While Celia showers, I unfold a bath towel, the same washed-out beige as the bedspread, and stretch it across the floor, then place in the middle of it the room's only chair. From here I can watch myself work in the darkened, damaged mirror. The room's lighting is terrible, but it will have to do.

I know that Celia might be lying. She claims she is innocent but has yet to offer any conclusive proof. And I am reminded of what she herself said earlier, that we humans are unfathomable. We barely even know ourselves. What can I do? I can take a leap of faith and believe her. Twenty years of friendship must count for something.

Celia soon emerges from the bathroom, in jeans but naked from the waist up, with her hair darkly soaked and rivulets of water streaming down her face. A hand towel curled around her shoulders covers her breasts but stops short of the ribs visible just below. She appears so ghostly pale, I gasp.

"The hot water felt lovely." She cocks her head and sweeps inside her ear with a corner of the towel. "Been ages since I had a proper shower."

I beckon her to the chair, where she collapses heavily, kicking out her feet. "Sit up straight." I tap her shoulder. "Square your shoulders and lift your chin."

Dutifully, she complies. "Can you manage with your broken hand?"

"I'll do my best." I comb through the tangles of her damaged hair, teasing out the tiny knots.

Her eyes drift closed. "I'll be relieved to go to the police," she says softly, folding her hands in her lap. "The last few months have been exhausting."

"I can't even imagine." My voice is strangely hoarse as I add, "It's not much longer now."

I reach for the scissors, but before I can make the first cut she stops my hand midair.

"Keep in mind," she says, clutching my fist, "I will never forgive you if you render me hideous."

I smile. "Like *that* could ever happen."

"All right then"—she nods solemnly and releases my hand—"you may continue."

I begin cutting with the scissors in my right hand and her hair pinched between the swollen fingers of my left. My initial snips are jagged and uneven, but my technique improves as I continue. Neither of us speaks and the only sounds are the snip of the busy scissors, the electric hum from the TV in the adjoining room, and occasional furtive footsteps in the corridor.

"Celia, I have to tell you something," I whisper, breaking the spell. "I lost your manuscript."

"My manuscript?"

"*The Harmony Argument*. When I fell at the station." I stumble over my words. "You must have a backup copy. Tell me where it is and I'll get it to your agent—"

She raises her hand to stop me. "Don't worry, Dayle. It's not important."

"But you spent years on that book."

"I know." She sighs. "But my passion for writing has dissipated. If it ever truly existed at all. You're the real writer, Dayle—not me. And you must write more." Her voice becomes sharp and insistent. "Serious books, to complement your fabulous spy novels. Promise you'll write another. And that you'll base one of the characters on me. But give her massive tits, of course."

"Of course." I smile, gazing down at the folds of Celia's abdomen, the bridge of her nose, the fading scar upon her cheek. The notch of her throat bounces when she swallows and the ridges of her collarbones rise with each breath. She appears so angular and exposed that her skin seems a mere formality, a transparent paper veil barely obscuring the secret activity beneath.

We were lovers so briefly; for such a short time, this body belonged to me, moved beneath me, responded to my needs and commands. We had been friends, platonic friends, for years, even though she came out in high school and I followed a few years later, during sophomore year of college. Still, it wasn't until after grad school, when we shared our flat in London and were both emerging from bad breakups, that we explored the possibility of being more than friends. It was short-lived, a mere six weeks or so, and beautiful, all her tough sarcasm and swagger falling away in moments of thrilling, breathtaking intimacy, but we soon realized that the things that made us great friends prevented us from being great partners.

We managed to stay friends afterward, but our relationship was never quite the same, and it was only a few weeks later that I got a great job offer and moved back home to Chicago.

I comb the hair from Celia's crown over her forehead to her chin, securing it between my swollen fingers. As I raise the scissors, Celia stiffens and one eye drops open. "Tell me you are not giving me a fringe."

"I am."

"I'll look twelve," she protests.

"You'll look more like me."

She sighs heavily. "Very well then."

I snip the bangs to just above her eyebrows and straight across her forehead. She instantly looks years younger as her high cheekbones become the focal point of her heart-shaped face.

"Oh God, you seem pleased," she complains, brushing the shorn hair from her lap. "It must be dreadful."

"See for yourself." I help her up and guide her to the mirror, where she considers her reflection. "It's supposed to be a bob." I cup the hair beneath her ear with my good hand. "It should curl under more."

Celia won't admit she likes the haircut, but I can tell she is pleased as she squints at her reflection, tugging the blunted ends so they settle against her skin.

"It's not bad." She cranes closer to the glass. "In fact, I'm rather impressed. You were always one of those annoying people who is naturally good at everything."

While Celia retreats to the bathroom to color her hair, I crawl into the foul-smelling bed and click through the TV channels. There isn't much on at this hour, a brief update on the thwarted terrorist attack, soccer news from the Premier League, a recap of the day's developments in parliament, and an old black-and-white movie starring David Niven. I don't even realize that I've fallen asleep until the bed jostles and my eyes fly open. Celia leans over me, reaching into the sheets.

"Sorry," she apologizes, standing upright with fists on hips. "Didn't mean to wake you. I was looking for the remote."

I squint, trying to clear my vision. Celia's hair has been transformed from a flat, lifeless blond to a vivid, inky black. Not only is her hair now black, it has been dried and styled to frame her face. Her pale skin, cleaned of makeup, looks freshly scrubbed and shining. Barefoot, she wears a pair of shorts and my purple Northwestern University T-shirt.

She notices me looking at the shirt. "I hope you don't mind I borrowed this." She stretches the shirt's hem over her bare knees. "Nicked it from your suitcase."

"No, that's okay." I yawn. "How long was I asleep?"

"Not very long." She pats my leg and smiles. "You're knackered—get some rest."

I sit up, forgetting that my hand is broken until the cast jams the mattress, unleashing a dagger of pain. "Damn." I bolt forward, clutching my arm.

"Are you all right?" Celia looks worried.

"I'll be fine." I breathe deeply, willing the pain away. Gradually, it ebbs to a dull throb. "You know what? I'm really hungry."

She shakes her head. "We won't find much to eat this time of night."

"Look in my backpack." I nod toward the luggage stacked against the wall. "I brought what I could find from your flat."

She steps to the backpack, unzips it, and feels around inside. "A golden syrup cake...a can of lager," she announces, placing each item on the bed. "And some sort of meat pie I don't ever recall buying." She scowls at me over her shoulder. "This came from my flat?"

"Yep."

"Well, if we don't survive the night, we'll know why." She turns over the plastic wrapper. "I don't even see a best-by date."

"That must mean we'll be okay."

She rolls her eyes. "You always were an optimist."

We sit cross-legged on the bed with our humble meal on the hand towel between us. I reach for the cake but can't open it with my swollen fingers.

"Here, let me." Celia unwraps the cake and tears it into bite-size chunks. When I reach for a piece she shakes her head and beckons me closer. "Here"—she nods—"allow me."

I lean forward and open my mouth. She places the morsel on my tongue, holding her palm beneath my chin. The cake is delicious, sweet and spongy with a golden liquid core. She takes the second section for herself and then pushes the remainder toward my knee.

"Too delicious," she pronounces, eyes closed as she smiles with satisfaction. "Ought to be illegal."

As we eat we can hear the amorous exultations of the couple in the room next door. What began as an innocent romp soon escalates in intensity, rattling the walls. *Yes, Leslie, yes!*

Celia and I giggle, nearly choking on our cake.

Oh yes! Oh yes!

We pause, mid-chew, eyes locked, waiting for the inevitable.

Lesssss-leee! Yes!

Celia collapses backward in laughter, nearly falling off the bed. I grab the beer can before it rolls to the floor, then struggle to open it.

"Here—let me." Celia rights herself, grinding her bare heels into the dirty bedspread. I hand her the can and she holds it, arm's-length, and pops the tab. A crown of foam immediately bubbles over the top. Celia brings it quickly to her lips and siphons the foam, then takes a long swig for good measure.

"Here, drink this." She holds the can to my lips as I lean forward and sip, letting the lukewarm liquid settle, not just at the bottom of my stomach, but at the base of my soul.

"I'm going to miss spending time like this." Celia pins the can between her feet.

"Me too." The beer makes me belch and I press my forearm to my mouth, stifling the release.

"I always pictured us as old ladies someday, trotting off to bingo with our Zimmer frames." She takes the meat pie, cradling it in her palms. "Dayle, if there's a way to contact you, I will. When I'm on the other side, I mean."

"I know. I know you'll try."

Celia divides up the meat pie, which gives off a faintly gamey odor as the thick pastry shell is broken and a gelatinous brown gravy oozes forth. Celia places the pieces on the hand towel between our feet. "I'm so sorry, Dayle," she says quietly, shaking her head.

"Sorry for what?"

"For not staying in touch as I should have. All that time we let slip away. We can never get it back now."

"It's as much my fault as yours." I take a small bite of pie, then set the rest aside.

"Did we even have a row? A falling out?"

"I don't think so. Things just…changed."

She frowns. "I never rang you after…you know."

My breath catches. *Celia—don't. Not now.*

"Your mum e-mailed me afterward, asked me to get in touch. And I meant to. I truly did." She releases a deep sigh. "But then I didn't."

"Lots of people didn't," I say softly.

"Even so, that doesn't make it right." She bites her bottom lip, unable to look me in the eye. "I thought of ringing you so many times, even picked up the phone, but didn't know what to say. The truth is, I was afraid you might weep. And I'd feel embarrassed. Pathetic, isn't it? All the stupid, foolish things we tell ourselves, when all we really need to do is step up and be human."

"It's okay. It's over now," I whisper, even though I know that for me, it will never be over.

She sips the beer, then nestles the can in the crook of her knee. "I can't fathom what you must have gone through."

"It was pretty horrible," I finally say after searching for the words. *Let's not talk about this. Not tonight.*

"At least you had your faith."

"I suppose so." My mind flashes to the couple in the adjoining room, Leslie and his friend, perhaps just now falling asleep in each other's arms.

"I always admired your faith, even though I didn't share it." Celia takes the wrapper from the meat pie and smooths it with her fingertips. Her hazel eyes, dilated by the low light, seem hollow and far away.

"I remember you and your mum and dad getting all dressed up on a Sunday and driving to that little Lutheran church, the wooden one with the tall white steeple, off that country highway." She smiles gently at the memory. "When I first came to the States I couldn't believe people still did that, put on their Sunday best and went to church, where they sang hymns and praised the Lord and whatnot. I found it so quaint then, but there have been many times in my life since that I have wished for such certainty."

My skin prickles. "I wouldn't call it certainty."

She shrugs. "Certainty, faith, belief—however you label it. The confidence that your baby is in a better place."

"And what place could be better than with me?" I blurt out. "Me—the mother who loved him?"

Celia looks up in surprise. "I didn't mean—"

"I don't know where my son is, I only know where he isn't." I've held it in for so long the words, set free, tumble out in a rush. "He isn't in my arms, or on my lap, or in his high chair or his crib or his bouncy seat. The world is full of places he's supposed to be. Places I created just for him. Don't you understand? He is everywhere and nowhere, all at once. How can he be so here, so present that I sense him all around me, and yet so utterly and completely gone?" My voice breaks and I stop.

Celia stares at me in horror, her pale cheeks pulsing red. "I'm sorry, Dayle. I didn't mean to be insensitive."

"No, it's okay." I swallow hard. "It's good, really. I rarely get to talk about him. Like you said, it makes people uncomfortable."

She looks wounded. "I'm so much more than *people*, Dayle."

"I know." I glance at the clock and see that it's almost six a.m. "Look, it's already morning," I say. "We should try to get some sleep while we still can. I'm gonna go wash up."

She places her hand kindly on my knee and the pressure of her touch makes me ache. "Are you certain you're all right?"

"I'm fine."

I climb off the bed and hurry into the bathroom, where I am free to weep, silently, so Celia cannot hear. I turn away from the mirror, so I don't see the swollen face leaking tears and the bruise surfacing beneath my left eye, where my cheek hit the Tube platform.

I struggle out of my clothes and into the T-shirt and sweatpants I wore earlier, then manage to wash my face and brush my teeth, all while averting my eyes from the mirror.

When I slip quietly out of the bathroom I discover that Celia has fallen asleep atop the bed. Her newly black, blunt-cut hair is tucked behind her right ear and she lies on her left side, knees pulled to her chest and hands folded beneath her cheek in a position resembling prayer.

It is 6:21 a.m. I had hoped we might share the bed for a few hours of sleep before we leave for the police station, but looking at Celia resting so peacefully, I can't bear to wake her and ask her to make room for me. So instead I cover her with an extra blanket from the closet and turn off the lights, leaving the bathroom light on and the door inched open, so only enough light fills the room to leave the biggest objects visible; visible, but drained of color and detail, reduced to outlines, vague shadows, and shapes. Even now the room is mostly dark, the only natural light coming from the small street-level window. A narrow shaft of light cast from the bathroom creeps across the carpet and rises up the side of the bed, illuminating the smooth serenity of Celia's sleeping face.

I take the chair and straddle it, folding my arms and resting my chin on my cast. From here I watch Celia sleep, marking the way her forehead crinkles and her sparse eyebrows rise, meet, then relax as she exhales. In the absence of light, the noises outside seem both magnified and menacing: the rattle of metal bars opening over storefronts, a rare bird chirping, the splash of tires squealing through standing water.

For a moment Celia and I are thirteen again, bundled into army cots in a cabin at Camp Minnehowee in northern

Wisconsin. Our two cabinmates, a shy Amish girl from Ohio and a 240-pound tattooed juvenile delinquent from Indianapolis, sleep soundly while Celia and I clutch our flashlights and hold our breath as we listen for the distant cries of herons, wolves, and loons. Celia is scared into wide-eyed silence; this big-city girl has never slept outside in a wooden A-frame, so exposed to nature. She finds the vast darkness terrifying, the featureless deep of the clear night sky where black meets black, obliterating any kind of horizon.

"It's all right," I reassured her, "close your eyes and go to bed. I'll stay up and keep watch while you sleep." I only knew for certain she was sleeping by the subtle shift in the rhythm of her breathing.

Who is she? I wonder, staring at Celia now, across the room from me at the Bayswater bed-and-breakfast. Who is she, really? Is she Celia the liberator, the deliverer, the freer of souls? Or is she someone who profited financially from the sex trafficking of young women and girls? Can anyone ever truly know another human being? And if not, how can we act without that knowledge? Can faith alone ever be enough?

I vow to stay awake until it's time to leave, guarding Celia's silent, slumbering form. I will be steadfast. Faithful. I will not close my eyes. No. Not this time.

❖

My body jerks sharply, startling me from sleep, from that achingly vivid dream in which a baby cries nearby. The closer I get to consciousness the more he retreats until, when I open my eyes and reach for him, he is gone. Pain shoots through my arm.

I squint, struggling to make out the clock. Even though the room is still dark, it's 7:45 a.m. "Celia?" I mumble sleepily. "Get up. We gotta go." As my eyes focus, I realize the bed is empty, save for a jumble of blankets and sheets. Hoping against hope I glance toward the bathroom, but the door is open and the light is off.

Oh my God, she's gone. Celia's gone. The realization tumbles through me like bricks falling into a well. How could I have been so stupid? She was guilty all along, and now she's escaped.

CHAPTER TWENTY

Thursday
7:51 a.m.

My mind races as I consider what to do. Call the police? Callaway? Edwina? And what, exactly, would I tell them? As I rise from the chair I see on the desk behind me a scrap of paper, torn from a notepad and secured beneath last night's empty beer can. I grab the note and read it, hand shaking:

Dayle—You looked so knackered, I couldn't bear to wake you. Meet me at the tomb, 9.15. I'm off to Hope House to give Sophie the £5000. I don't need it now, and it's the least I can do.
—Celia XXX

I feel a strange mixture of hope and dread. Is she serious about donating the money to Sophie's charity? Or is she hoping to buy precious time by sending me off on a pointless journey to Highgate while she quietly leaves the country? There's only one way to find out—make my way to the cemetery and hope she shows up. Or do I hope she *doesn't* show up? Do I want her to have gotten away, even if she is guilty?

I shower as best I can with my broken hand, holding the cast outside the curtain so it won't get wet, then dress quickly and grab Celia's duffel bag and my backpack and head upstairs to the lobby. It's 8:22 a.m. and as I step outside, the streets between Bayswater and Queensway are stirring to life. The souvenir shops, noodle houses, and bureaux de change are filling quickly with rich Japanese tourists, college students on spring break, and steely eyed Russians hustling cheap knock-off luggage from storefronts and street corners.

The sky is misty, verging on rain, while a trace of fog lingers, curling like a nervous housecat around lampposts, traffic lights, and the wrought-iron fencing that lines Hyde Park. Even with the fog, the chilled morning air contains an unsullied freshness, a buoyancy just waiting to be brought down. One day, one ordinary day, just the simple movement of the sun across the sky, can change your life more than you ever imagine.

❖

In the cab on the way to Highgate, my mind is tense and anxious, focused on Celia, but also on Callaway, picturing her greasy hair and beady eyes. Will she be there waiting, outside the cemetery gates? Or will she wait until after the handoff to take Celia into custody? Or will she keep her promise and not show up until Celia reaches Euston Station, supposedly on the way to Ireland? Why is Callaway so determined to get Celia, anyway? If Celia is just a small fish, as Callaway insisted, why devote so much of her time and resources to finding her? What's in it for Callaway? Suddenly an awful thought occurs— what if *Callaway* is working with Gregorovich? Instantly, yesterday's events are cast in a different, more sinister, light.

Oh my God—all the elements were there, if only I had paid attention:

Callaway searching Celia's flat after her initial investigation was supposedly complete, claiming to be double-checking something.

Callaway insisting on interviewing me at the hospital after my accident, even though the police station was only a few blocks away.

Callaway pressing me to describe the person who pushed me, even though I didn't see anyone. Was she actually behind my accident and feared I'd seen too much?

The pictures she showed me in Celia's flat were emotionally manipulative but offered little concrete evidence of wrongdoing by Celia. Celia exchanging money with Gregorovich? That could have been Celia paying him to release Anastasia, as Celia claimed. And how was Callaway so fortunate as to get that photo in the first place? In the right place at the right time? Or had Gregorovich told her exactly where and when the handoff would take place?

Celia is in more danger than either of us realized. I've got to reach her before Callaway does.

I tell the cabbie to step on it. As we approach the cemetery, I have him drop me at the top of Swain's Lane, a steep, winding one-way road that divides the two sides of the massive Highgate Cemetery. Once I have hurried past the old pub and the mechanic's garage at the top of the lane, the road narrows as dark brick walls rise up on either side, marking the cemetery's outer perimeters.

Thick trees overhead throw a dense net of shadows across the road below, creating a choked and claustrophobic atmosphere that sets my nerves on edge. An occasional car whizzes past, and each time I fear it's Callaway.

Ahead I can see where the trees break as the brick walls give way to the entrances to the two sides of the cemetery, the East Cemetery on my left and the West on the right.

The West Cemetery entrance is marked by a massive Main Gate, a brick fortress with rounded turrets and arched glass windows. I pay a small donation to enter and the attendant, a bored-looking man in his twenties, sets aside the textbook he'd been reading and waves me through the black iron gate, which swings closed behind me with a deep shudder that echoes through my body before settling in my broken hand, which vibrates long after the rest of me has stilled.

This is the first I have been inside a cemetery since Rory died. We buried him at the church that Celia remembered, the little Lutheran one with the tall white steeple, just off the country highway. Rory is buried beside my father, in the plot that had been reserved for my mother, with a headstone already engraved with her name and the year of her birth. *Four pounds, seven ounces. He lived for fifty-three minutes. His coffin was thirty-six inches long.* The numbers feel meaningless but they rush through my head nonetheless.

Just inside the cemetery's main gate is a broad open circle, elegantly paved and rimmed on the far side by a crescent-shaped colonnade with narrow, tombstone-shaped doorways. I hurry across the paved circle and through a doorway in the middle of the colonnade. Then I mount a stone staircase that takes me into the gently rolling grounds of the cemetery proper, where the ancient and more contemporary dead lie side by side, resting for all eternity beneath everything from simple stone crosses and modest grave markers to gigantic crypts, vaults, and mausoleums, many intricately carved and featuring elaborate, even garish, statuary of dogs, angels, cherubs, harps.

Highgate Cemetery is a strange and mysterious place. Built in the 1830s, it covers thirty-seven acres and has more than 53,000 graves holding the remains of more than 170,000 people. The atmosphere is certifiably spooky Victorian Gothic, thanks to the cemetery's official policy of managed neglect, allowing the grounds to remain wildly unmanicured, overrun with trees, vines, shrubs, and wildflowers that threaten to suffocate the countless tumbledown, crumbling, ramshackle graves.

I appear to be the cemetery's only visitor as I take one in the maze of many narrow, winding, muddy paths that cut through the dense vegetation toward the center of the cemetery. The fog, which had thinned to the lightness of a human breath back in Bayswater, still lingers here, farther north and at a higher altitude. This fog is in no hurry to lift as it kisses cold marble statues and embraces lonely gravestones, some untouched for decades by human hands.

Callaway could be on the way, I think, as a gust of damp wind whistles around my ears. Or she might be waiting, even now. I've got to get to Celia before she does. I quicken my pace as I move down the hillside and deeper into the cemetery, where the light barely pierces the tangled masses of brambles, holly, and thick wiry shrubs.

I approach the Egyptian Avenue, one of the cemetery's best-known landmarks, and enter a dark descending passageway beneath a great stone arch carved into the hillside, overgrown with ropy vines and cascades of ivy and marked on either side with obelisks. A chill darts up my spine as I hurry through the damp, shadowy tunnel lined with vaults, each holding a dozen ancient coffins. The vaults are separated by stone columns capped with carvings of lotus buds, extending the eerie theme.

The tunnel opens into the Circle of Lebanon, a sunken ring of elaborate Greco-Egyptian-style vaults and catacombs, twenty feet below ground level and fully exposed to the sky. In the middle of the circle stands the majestic Cedar of Lebanon tree around whose roots the circle was carved and which predates the cemetery by hundreds of years.

I can't remember exactly where Radclyffe Hall's tomb is located, so I work my way counterclockwise around the circle's damp dirt path, moving between the massive stone vaults lining the ring's outer edge, each sized, shaped, and designed like a small Gothic chapel, and the inner rim's catacombs, with their dark recessed iron doors set deep into the earth.

Roughly halfway around the circle, I turn the corner and there is Cecelia Frost waiting for me, standing in the shallow entrance to a vault with the name *Mabel Veronica Batten* chiseled overhead. Mabel Batten was Radclyffe Hall's first lover and it is within her tomb that Radclyffe Hall is buried. At Celia's feet is a small white marble planter, engraved with *Radclyffe Hall* and holding a delicate bouquet of pink flowers.

Seeing me, Celia drops her cigarette and crushes it with her boot heel, then raises her arm in a silent salute. It is still a shock to see the bobbed black hair framing her pale skin and even features. Beneath her denim jacket she wears my Green Bay Packers sweatshirt, borrowed from my suitcase.

My heart pounds as I rush toward her, my feet turning up clumps of damp dark soil. "Celia," I pant when I reach her. "What did you mean when you said you were guilty of enough other things?"

She ducks back into the doorway, eyes narrowing. "What?"

"Last night." I gulp for air, bending at the waist. "When I told you about Callaway and the photos. You said you never took payoffs from Gregorovich, but you were guilty of enough other things. What other things?"

She stiffens, jutting out her chin. "Dayle, what the hell is going on?"

Catching my breath, I speak more slowly. "Celia—I need to know. What else have you done?"

She folds her arms. "Nothing audacious. Just bent a few rules."

I turn, glance over my shoulder, then look past Celia, past the dark doorways that stare out like hollow eyes from the curved circle of tombs. "I need specifics," I insist.

She rolls her eyes. "Fine. Let's see—crossed into Ukraine on forged papers when I couldn't get a transit visa. Sold a blood diamond and gave the proceeds to a clinic in Sierra Leone. Slashed the tires on a van meant to traffic underage girls from Marseille to Rotterdam. Shook hands with evil people and told myself it was for a greater good." Her face softens. "But I'm done with all that, Dayle. I want a fresh start. I want to feel clean again. There are other ways to be of use in this world." She pauses. "Now tell me what the hell is going on."

"I believe Callaway is working with Gregorovich and they want you out of the way."

She inhales sharply. "What?"

"There's no time to explain. We've got to get you out of England."

I motion her away from the tomb's entrance but she stands her ground. "How?" she demands.

"By exchanging identities. I'll be you and you'll be me."

She shakes her head so rapidly the blunt black ends of her hair strike her cheek. "You *can't* be serious."

"I am. With your hair cut and colored, we look enough alike, at least from a distance, to pull it off. You'll take my flight to Chicago as Dayle Salvesen and I'll be Cecelia Frost for as long as possible." I slip the backpack from my shoulder and push it toward her. "Take this. Inside are my passport, driver's license, credit cards, cash, and the details for an e-ticket to Chicago. British Airways Flight 1544 out of Heathrow, leaving at twelve fifty. Be on that flight."

"But—"

"When you land at O'Hare, take a cab to my condo. The address is on my driver's license. I'll get a message to Mom, letting her know what's happened. She'll help you get settled until I get back."

"But the police will realize rather quickly you're not me," she argues.

"I know. I just want to buy enough time for you to catch that flight. We don't know what kind of false evidence Callaway might have. She may have convinced others that you're working with the traffickers. If you're here, you're in danger."

"But you're in danger too."

"Not as much as you are." I force a wry smile. "Besides— think how cool this will sound in the next *Assignment* novel." I fight my arms out of my jacket and motion for Celia to do the same. I struggle into her faded denim jacket while she slips on my green London Fog.

"Okay," I say, breathless. "One last thing."

"What?"

"This." I hold out my plaster cast and grasp it with my other hand.

Celia gasps. "Bloody hell!" Her face pales as she steps back in horror.

"You've got to help me. Please, Celia. It's the only way."

CHAPTER TWENTY-ONE

Thursday
9:15 a.m.

I bear down and pull. The pain is so intense, I feel nauseous. "Help me, Celia," I plead. "If my arm swells, the cast'll never come off."

I motion for her to grab hold above my knuckles while I push from below. "Okay," I say when we're both latched on tightly. "On three. Ready?"

She nods, looking queasy.

"Okay. One, two, three!" I push while she pulls. After several agonizing seconds of stubborn resistance, the cast releases and I stumble backward, blinded by pain. My broken hand feels electrified, as if I've plunged it into a bucket of stars.

"Are you all right?" The cast sways gently between Celia's fingertips.

"I think so." I rise to my knees and then sit back on my heels in the dirt, cradling my arm. The bones below my shoulder have turned to jelly; even my lips quiver. "Put it on," I pant, looking up at her. "You're so thin—it should slide right on."

With a nod she pushes up her sleeve and thrusts her left arm into the cast. It fits easily, stopping just below her elbow.

I struggle to my feet and Celia hands me the red duffel bag, which I heave over my shoulder, centering the weight against my ribs.

"Okay, let's go." I struggle to breathe through the pain as my arm goes numb at my side.

"Wait." Celia turns to the plaque affixed to the inner wall beside the entrance to the tomb. It reads, *Radclyffe Hall 1943*, and then beneath: *And, if God choose, I shall but love thee better after death. Una.*

Una was Una Troubridge, Mabel Batten's cousin who became Radclyffe Hall's lover after Mabel died. Una had planned to be buried in the vault alongside Mabel and Radclyffe, but she died unexpectedly in Rome and was buried in Rome's English Cemetery, her written instructions for burial not discovered until afterward. Her coffin in Rome was inscribed simply with the words, *Una Vincenzo Troubridge, the friend of Radclyffe Hall.*

"Come on, Celia, *now*," I urge her. "Before Callaway gets here."

"Wait. Just a moment longer." Celia, her face suddenly soft and strangely dreamy, caresses each carved letter on the plaque with her finger as if it were a loved one's cheek, then tenderly straightens the bouquet of pink flowers in the planter at her feet, just in front of the tomb's dark latticed door.

"Very well." She stands and surveys her handiwork with satisfaction, pressing the plaster cast against her lip. "*Now* we can go."

We stride side by side along the circular dirt path, past the ring of stately vaults and corniced catacombs to a broad stone stairway, then mount the vivid green, moss-softened steps and emerge from the circle at ground level. I look around anxiously, surveying the dense, almost primordial, vegetation, rich with a lush, dark decadence, almost anti-English in its lack of order and restraint. There's no sign of Callaway or the police anywhere. Nothing but row after row of crosses, headstones, and ancient, sunken graves tipped sullenly toward the center of the earth.

"Back to the front gate." I touch Celia's sleeve and whisper in her ear, "Not too fast, not too slow. Steady steps."

She nods grimly as we trek down yet another winding, muddy pathway, overrun with knotted grasses and muscular, sinuous weeds. The graves and mausoleums seem older and more elaborate in this part of the cemetery; we weave between towering Celtic crosses with encircled arms and chiseled statues of angels, saints, and garland-draped urns. Death is everywhere here—memorialized and normalized by Victorian Londoners for whom death was never distant, and no one was ever safe from that grim shadow passing always overhead.

"When we get through the front gate, we separate," I tell Celia. "Go to Archway station. Get on the Tube, but get off after the first stop or two—somewhere unexpected, somewhere neither of us would be likely to go. Grab a cab to Heathrow, but don't check in until the gate's about to close. Lie low, be careful, you'll be fine."

Scattered thoughts careen through my head, bouncing and ricocheting like carnival bumper cars. "When you land at O'Hare, take a cab to my condo. Call my mom and explain what's going on, in case I can't reach her before you arrive. Tell her I love her and I'll be home soon."

Celia tucks her chin to her chest as her scuffed leather boots squish through the mud. The path here is so narrow that drooping vines tickle our faces as we push forward. "You don't have to do this," she offers softly. "I'm willing to go to the police, Callaway notwithstanding."

"I know. But I want to do this. I *need* to do this. If I'd believed you all along, we wouldn't be in this situation." My mind races and my arm aches; the very air seems to burnish my bruised and tender skin. "Hug my cats when you get to my condo. Hamlet and Yorick. They have similar black-and-white markings, but Hamlet is fatter. They like to be picked up, turned over, and have their tummies rubbed."

Celia swivels to face me, her hazel eyes wide and surprised. "Are you serious?"

"Yep."

"Dayle, you really *must* get out more often."

I allow myself a brief, tight smile, then motion to continue.

❖

We're halfway back to the front gate when I sense that something isn't right. It's not that we're being watched or followed. It feels more like something is encroaching, closing in. A circle narrowing, constricting—a breath held too long and anxious for release. I feel movement all around us in the whispering oak and chestnut trees and in the shadows cast by massive granite vaults and bashful stone-faced angels gazing down from giant crosses. I think I see something—a glint of metal, a brief flash of silvery light. I'm sure it's nothing.

My steps quicken and Celia struggles to keep pace. "My condo has two bedrooms," I continue. "Feel free to sleep in the master bedroom. The other room…belongs to Rory."

The heavy vegetation thins, the sky lightens, and in the mist up ahead, a man—average height, Caucasian, late twenties—advances toward us on the path. Highgate normally receives a steady stream of visitors, but this man doesn't look like a sightseer, dressed in jeans, sneakers, and a hooded gray sweatshirt with the hood pulled forward, obscuring his face. As he glances up, his hands slip quickly into the front pocket of his sweatshirt. Please just let him be a Candee Cronin fan, I think absurdly.

Celia too seems to sense that something is wrong. The man draws steadily closer. His eyes, two beads shining blackly beneath the peak of his hood, emerge from the shadow to focus on us briefly before glancing down.

Keep moving; keep walking. Don't do anything suspicious. Each minute off the clock brings Celia closer to freedom. It's not much longer now.

The man is almost upon us. We could break away and make a run for it. But there's no way out of the cemetery other than through the front gate, and we don't want our exit to cause a commotion. If we can just get past this guy, we'll be fine.

"Be careful," I whisper to Celia. "I'm not sure about this one."

Celia nods gravely, drawing her arms to her sides.

In a matter of moments the man is upon us. As I make eye contact, his eyelids flicker and he looks away. His sweatshirt brushes my shoulder, jostling the duffel bag as he barrels past me with long, forceful strides. I am just about to breathe a sigh of relief when he turns suddenly, grabs my shoulder, and spins me around. I stumble out of his grasp, dropping the duffel bag to the ground.

Celia screams. I turn in time to see the knife, withdrawn with a glimmer from the pouch of his sweatshirt. The man swings at my arm, slashing the denim sleeve. "Run!" I yell at Celia. "Go! Get out of here, now!"

I duck and pivot as the man makes another rapid slash at my side, this time missing me by inches. I close my eyes as he swings again. Celia angles between us and pushes me behind her, shielding me with her body.

"Leave it out!" she screams as the man again raises the knife. Celia rears back and smashes his face with the plaster cast on her arm, ramming her hand into his nose, nearly knocking him off his feet as he, stunned, stumbles backward. Blood pours from his nose, streaking his lips and dribbling from his chin. Celia knocks the knife from his hand and it falls to the ground, where it lands with a dull thud, glinting against the damp soil.

Celia lunges toward the knife but the man is faster as he bends and grasps it, plunging it into his pocket. Then he turns and runs away, back down the winding path, a dark form darting quickly out of view.

"He's gone," I whisper, doubled over and struggling to breathe. "But I think I'm okay." I touch the slashed sleeve of my jacket where the denim has split, leaving only a riot of white thread remaining. "He didn't get any skin. How about you?"

"Still in one piece," she pants, tenderly testing her ribs.

"Why didn't you run?" I ask. "You could have gotten away."

"And leave you to fend for yourself? Not bloody likely." She shakes her head, still panting. "That knife was meant for me. For Celia, not for Dayle, the one with the cast on her arm." She waves the plaster-cast arm in weak surrender, then opens her jacket, revealing two tiny petals of blood blossoming in the sweatshirt's bottom hem.

"Celia—look."

She glances down and grimaces, her mouth a determined downward slash. "What do you know? Looks like the bastard got me after all."

"Let me see." I reach for the sweatshirt but she withdraws quickly, as if my fingers were flame. "It's okay," I say gently. "I'll just take a peek." I step closer and carefully lift the sweatshirt, which is glued to the T-shirt beneath with a dark sticky circle of blood.

Celia's face pales.

"Don't worry," I reassure her. "Just hold still." She stands, stiff and rigid, while I search for the wound, sweeping her skin until I find a two-inch gash on the right side of her abdomen, just above her hip.

The slit, though small, weeps steady beads of blood that gather in her waistband. I slide my finger into the wound, trying to gauge its depth and staunch the flow, but the blood rises quickly, covering my finger. Celia's knees weaken as air rushes from her lungs. "Dayle…?"

I clutch her shoulder, trying to hold her upright. "Just hold on, okay? Be strong." Information from the third grade, gathered in pursuit of the Brownies first-aid badge, races through my mind. *Keep her covered, keep her calm, keep her warm. Raise her head and legs.* How? And with what?

She starts to tremble, her pale shocked face stricken and desperate.

I've got to do something. Now.

"Come on," I say, my voice shaking. "Let's go sit down." I hike the duffel bag over my shoulder and with my arm around Celia's waist we stumble like drunks, off the narrow path and into the sacred space where the grass is thickly matted and the graves so close and cloistered their ghosts can gossip easily, leaning in to whisper, mouth to ear.

I nod toward a patch of clover nestled between two jagged headstones and edged by an ancient oak tree. Celia, anguished, leaves my side and sinks slowly to the base of the tree, which is cushioned by ferns and small yellow flowers. "Okay?" I ask, looking down at her.

"Never better," she whispers bitterly, struggling to steady her shaking legs.

"Press your hand firmly to the wound," I advise her. "As hard as you can manage, all right?"

She nods grimly, hunching forward and bearing down against the pain.

I reach into the duffel bag and pull out my cell phone, but get only a no-service message. Damn. Maybe I could get a signal somewhere else in the cemetery, but I can't leave Celia—not like this.

So I forgo the phone and duffel bag and instead drop to my knees beside her, feeling her sweaty forehead and clammy cheeks. Threads of blood unspool between her fingers, blackening the grass and staining the dark earth beneath her hip. This is happening too quickly—why is she losing so much blood?

"Right," I say confidently, fighting off my denim jacket and placing it on the damp ground beside me. Then I gently loosen Celia's clenched white knuckles, peeling back the shirt to check the wound.

"Bad?" she whispers through clenched teeth.

"No," I lie, re-covering the wound. "But you'll probably need a few stitches."

"Brilliant," she sputters. "*Another* scar."

"Don't worry—it'll be tiny." I lean back on my heels and look to the sky, to the dense but delicate web of tree braches darting and weaving overhead, and down to the neglected nearby graves of Lillian and Edward Chesterfield and their infant daughter, Clarrisa, born and died in April 1892, but help is not forthcoming. It occurs to me I should scream, I should call for help, I should do *something*. Celia needs me now.

"Come on, scoot over." Still on my knees I move behind Celia, wedging myself between her and the tree.

Her limbs stiffen. "What the hell?" she demands as a flare of anger briefly flames her cheeks.

"It's okay." I gently hook her waist with my good arm and center her between my legs. "Let's keep you warm till help arrives."

"Right. 'Cause they're *certain* to be here any moment."

"Come on—just let me help." I draw her backbone to my chest as I circle her quivering ribs. With my broken hand I drag the denim jacket closer and drape it across our bodies. "Better?" I ask, willing the heat of my body to pass into her.

"Yeah." Her breathing is rough, ragged. "*Just* spiffy."

I move my hand down to her wound, feeling the warm creep of blood filling the fabric and spreading between my fingers. This is so much worse than I imagined.

Celia winces and I smell fear rise from her neck, from the damp back of her collar. Then her jaw softens and her eyelids flutter, even as she struggles to stay annoyed. It wouldn't be like Celia to make this easy for me.

"Just relax," I say gently, stroking her arm and breathing through the blunt softness of her newly blackened hair, which is cool to the touch and still smells slightly of dye. I gaze down at her face, her ghost of a black eye, the shadow of a damaged cheek, and I let myself feel the familiar shape she carves into my arms, the warm settled weight of her torso, the notches of her spine nestled against my breastbone. I have missed her so much, I realize, have missed holding her like this.

"I'll take care of you, Celia," I promise, brushing aside

her short, black, roughly cut bangs and hoping she'll forgive me for sounding sentimental. "You ferried so many people to safety. Let me carry you now."

"Well aren't I the lucky one." Celia's raspy voice curls with sarcasm; she swallows hard to stem the tears. We share a silent understanding that life is leaving her quickly, leeching out of her pores, or escaping stealthily, like steam rising from a kettle.

I steel my voice with false bravado. "Celia, listen. Just hang on. I'll get you out of this somehow, I swear." She nods quickly, closing her eyes, but as I shift my hip against the cold, hard ground, I can feel Celia's heart surface from somewhere deep inside her, a faint, frantic tapping, like a prisoner desperate to escape his cell.

The fog begins to lift, rising above the graves and throwing them into high relief as the chill morning air fills suddenly with birdsong—goldfinch, sparrow, starling, lark. Highgate, this garish Victorian death-obsessed theme park, holds so much more life than I first realized—not just songbirds but foxes, rabbits, badgers, doves. I want to share this realization with Celia, but she is long past caring now.

Suddenly agitated, Celia shivers and lifts her chin, her breathing light and rapid as her eyes fly open and her lips flush with blue. "Daddy?" she calls out, desperate as a little girl. "Daddy! Where are you?"

"It's okay, Celia. Just hang on." I gaze into her empty black eyes, all pupil, staring up at me in stunted sorrow. We share the same thought: This cannot be happening. This cannot be happening to *her*. She is too proud, too arrogant to die so quietly, in the corner of a desolate cemetery on a foggy morning in March. "It's okay," I coo, softly rocking her back and forth. "I've got you in my arms."

Her face contorts in pain and her bluish lips pucker. "Dayle, I want my dad."

"I know. And he'll be here soon, I promise. Just stay calm." She sighs as I pull her closer, tightening my grip around her ribs.

I came to London just over twenty-four hours ago with only one thing on my mind: seeing Celia. Not the conference, not the keynote speech, just Celia. I had hoped to rekindle that fallow friendship and return home enriched with more tales of my bold, brilliant, fearless friend. I never dreamed that my journey here held a second, secret purpose: to do for Celia what I had failed to do for my son—to hold her in her final moments and see her safely to the other side, to deliver her gently into the arms of a great someone. *Steady. Rest now. We are so, so close to home.*

As I press my lips against Celia's temple, a stone angel rises behind me and veils us in the shadow of his feathery wings. The sky separates; shards of light pierce the canopy of branches and leaves, casting dazzling patterns on the cemetery floor, where Celia and I huddle as if shipwrecked, marooned and helpless in a deep shifting sea of emerald green.

Suddenly three figures emerge from the foggy haze at the bottom of the path and sprint toward us, limbs hurtling like windmills as the ghostly shapes assume human form. "They're coming." Hope tightens my throat. "Help is almost here."

Celia moans.

As the figures draw closer, I see that it is Callaway, in heavy boots and her dirty trench coat, flanked by a uniformed police officer on either side.

Celia stirs to life as a tremor moves through her. "Dayle?" Her tongue is thick and she struggles to speak.

"Yes?"

"Don't tell them I was frightened."

Frightened? That's what she's worried about? "I won't." My voice is defiant. "Now just hold on."

"I can't." Her arms slide limply to her sides.

Callaway and the two men stumble to a stop just in front of us. All three are winded, gulping buckets of cold, damp air. "What the hell happened?" Callaway bends at the waist, hands on her hips as the two cops reach for Celia.

I turn Celia's ashen face away from them as her body spasms and then softens, relaxing in my arms. My cheeks burn as I look up. "You're too late," I say triumphantly. "Celia's safe, and you can never hurt her now."

EPILOGUE

Six months later
Chicago, Illinois

My suspicions about Detective Constable Andrea Callaway turned out to be correct: She was taking payoffs from Gregorovich in exchange for police protection. Gregorovich hated Celia's work and all she stood for, so he paid Callaway to have Celia eliminated.

Callaway had used the photographs to manipulate me that night in Celia's flat. There had never been any witness protection program with the promise of a new name and identity; Callaway's endgame was always to initiate Celia's death. And my own. Callaway, using the information I had provided, hired the man in the hooded sweatshirt to attack us at Highgate Cemetery that morning in March.

Callaway had assembled enough false evidence to make the case against Celia appear quite compelling, but once I told the police what I knew, Callaway's story unraveled rather dramatically. After being taken into custody, she provided details of our assailant's identity in exchange for what she hoped would be a lighter sentence. Both she and the man pleaded guilty and will spend many years in prison.

Following Callaway's arrest, the police determined that Celia had committed no crime. Therefore, I faced no charges for trying to help her leave England. After a series of interviews with the police and some assistance from the American Embassy, I was free to return home to Chicago.

Since I have been back, I have canceled my trip to Japan and had the contract for *Assignment: Tokyo* voided. Candee Cronin has taken an extended sabbatical so she might find herself as an author once again. Her fans are said to be quite disappointed. What few people know, however, is that Dayle Salvesen is working on a new book—a small literary novel about a shy teenage girl and her well-endowed friend trying to mount their own musical stage production of *Gulliver's Travels*.

I struggled for a long time deciding how best to honor Celia. She had offered the ultimate sacrifice, been willing to give up her life for my own. Ultimately I purchased a burned-out old factory and the surrounding brownfield on Chicago's Far South Side and invested $250,000 to build the Marguerite Alderton Memorial Women's Center. Celia, given her modesty, would not have wanted the center to bear her own name. So I gave it her mother's name instead, to memorialize a woman, long gone, whose name represented for Celia her hopes and dreams of a new life in America.

The Alderton Center, in one of the city's poorest neighborhoods, will provide disadvantaged, immigrant, and abused women with shelter, health care, job training, and other social services. And Celia will arrive from London in two weeks' time to run the center, once all her green card paperwork is approved.

Celia's knife wound, though serious, was not fatal, although it took numerous transfusions and hours of surgery to save her life, followed by weeks of a slow and painful recovery. Edwina and I saw her through the worst of it, keeping nightly vigil at her hospital bedside, where we slept in shifts so one of us would always be awake to watch over her. Celia was a terrible patient—rude and moody, refusing to eat and always quick to complain. But I must say, she has been left with a rather sexy little scar. And I have kept my promise; I never did tell anyone that she'd been frightened.

But Celia's survival, though miraculous, has also been bittersweet. The truth is that I lost Celia that morning at Highgate Cemetery, just not in the way I imagined. I lost the Celia of my childhood, my one-time lover, that sharp yet tender friend who introduced me to the wonders of Joy Division and jam butties, who encouraged me to write like my life depended on it, and who taught me to smoke in my grandmother's basement, with the stinky unfiltered Gauloises she had smuggled back from England in her suitcase, duty-free.

But even as I lost Cecelia Frost, I gained something much greater. When I held Celia close that morning among the graves, felt her slender curve of bone and the pressure of her spine against my sternum, I understood what my mother must have felt as she held my Rory, my doomed and precious son; as tiny as he was, his shape, his weight, his very essence, must have been immense and overwhelming. I know my mother hasn't told me everything about those moments, but someday she will. Just as someday I will tell Celia everything—when she is finally ready to listen, when at last she is able to hear.

Celia refuses to forgive me, of course, to forgive me for witnessing her weakness, and for never being able to see her exactly the same way as before. She revealed too much during those desperate, panicky moments inside Highgate Cemetery; her careful mask slipped and I caught a glimpse of her soul, saw her lost and scared and vulnerable, the little girl with the ice cream waiting patiently on the swing for the mother who would never return. She resents me for that now, and always will. But her resentment, this cleft in our relationship, is a small price to pay for her life, and it's a price I will pay gladly until the day I die. In the end, Cecelia Frost remains a mystery. But I find I am less and less a mystery to myself.

About the Author

Elizabeth Ridley was born and raised in Milwaukee, Wisconsin. She has a bachelor's degree in journalism from Northwestern University and a master's degree in creative writing from the University of East Anglia in Norwich, England, where she studied under former Poet Laureate Sir Andrew Motion. In 1994, she received a Hawthornden Fellowship to Hawthornden Castle in Lasswade, Scotland, and in 2011 she received a Literary Artist Fellowship from the Wisconsin Arts Board based on the first three chapters of *Searching for Celia*. *Searching for Celia* is her fifth novel. She lives in Milwaukee with her two cats, Claudius and Calpurnia, and is producing her first feature film, *Handle with Care*. www.elizabethridley.com.

Books Available from Bold Strokes Books

Hardwired by C.P. Rowlands. Award-winning teacher Clary Stone, and Leefe Ellis, manager of the homeless shelter for small children, stand together in a part of Clary's hometown that she never knew existed. (978-1-62639-351-6)

No Good Reason by Cari Hunter. A violent kidnapping in a Peak District village pushes Detective Sanne Jensen and lifelong friend Dr. Meg Fielding closer, just as it threatens to tear everything apart. (978-1-62639-352-3)

Romance by the Book by Jo Victor. If Cam didn't keep disrupting her life, maybe Alex could uncover the secret of a century-old love story, and solve the greatest mystery of all— her own heart. (978-1-62639-353-0)

Death's Doorway by Crin Claxton. Helping the dead can be deadly: Tony may be listening to the dead, but she needs to learn to listen to the living. (978-1-62639-354-7)

Searching for Celia by Elizabeth Ridley. As American spy novelist Dayle Salvesen investigates the mysterious disappearance of her ex-lover, Celia, in London, she begins questioning how well she knew Celia—and how well she knows herself. (978-1-62639-356-1)

The 45th Parallel by Lisa Girolami. Burying her mother isn't the worst thing that can happen to Val Montague when she returns to the woodsy but peculiar town of Hemlock, Oregon. (978-1-62639-342-4)

A Royal Romance by Jenny Frame. In a country where class still divides, can love topple the last social taboo and allow Queen Georgina and Beatrice Elliot, a working class girl, their happy ever after? (978-1-62639-360-8)

Bouncing by Jaime Maddox. Basketball Coach Alex Dalton has been bouncing from woman to woman, because no one ever held her interest, until she meets her new assistant, Britain Dodge. (978-1-62639-344-8)

Same Time Next Week by Emily Smith. A chance encounter between Alex Harris and the beautiful Michelle Masters leads to a whirlwind friendship, and causes Alex to question everything she's ever known—including her own marriage. (978-1-62639-345-5)

All Things Rise by Missouri Vaun. Cole rescues a striking pilot who crash-lands near her family's farm, setting in motion a chain of events that will forever alter the course of her life. (978-1-62639-346-2)

Riding Passion by D. Jackson Leigh. Mount up for the ride through a sizzling anthology of chance encounters, buried desires, romantic surprises, and blazing passion. (978-1-62639-349-3)

Love's Bounty by Yolanda Wallace. Lobster boat captain Jake Myers stopped living the day she cheated death, but meeting greenhorn Shy Silva stirs her back to life. (978-1-62639-334-9)

Just Three Words by Melissa Brayden. Sometimes the one you want is the one you least suspect. Accountant Samantha

Ennis has her ordered life disrupted when heartbreaker Hunter Blair moves into her trendy Soho loft. (978-1-62639-335-6)

Lay Down the Law by Carsen Taite. Attorney Peyton Davis returns to her Texas roots to take on big oil and the Mexican Mafia, but will her investigation thwart her chance at true love? (978-1-62639-336-3)

Playing in Shadow by Lesley Davis. Survivor's guilt threatens to keep Bryce trapped in her nightmare world unless Scarlet's love can pull her out of the darkness back into the light. (978-1-62639-337-0)

Soul Selecta by Gill McKnight. Soul mates are hell to work with. (978-1-62639-338-7)

The Revelation of Beatrice Darby by Jean Copeland. Adolescence is complicated, but Beatrice Darby is about to discover how impossible it can seem to a lesbian coming of age in conservative 1950s New England. (978-1-62639-339-4)

Twice Lucky by Mardi Alexander. For firefighter Mackenzie James and Dr. Sarah Macarthur, there's suddenly a whole lot more in life to understand, to consider, to risk…someone will need to fight for her life. (978-1-62639-325-7)

Shadow Hunt by L.L. Raand. With young to raise and her Pack under attack, Sylvan, Alpha of the wolf Weres, takes on her greatest challenge when she determines to uncover the faceless enemies known as the Shadow Lords. A Midnight Hunters novel. (978-1-62639-326-4)

Heart of the Game by Rachel Spangler. A baseball writer falls for a single mom, but can she ever love anything as much as she loves the game? (978-1-62639-327-1)

Getting Lost by Michelle Grubb. Twenty-eight days, thirteen European countries, a tour manager fighting attraction, and an accused murderer: Stella and Phoebe's journey of a lifetime begins here. (978-1-62639-328-8)

Prayer of the Handmaiden by Merry Shannon. Celibate priestess Kadrian must defend the kingdom of Ithyria from a dangerous enemy and ultimately choose between her duty to the Goddess and the love of her childhood sweetheart, Erinda. (978-1-62639-329-5)

The Witch of Stalingrad by Justine Saracen. A Soviet "night witch" pilot and American journalist meet on the Eastern Front in WW II and struggle through carnage, conflicting politics, and the deadly Russian winter. (978-1-62639-330-1)

Pedal to the Metal by Jesse J. Thoma. When unreformed thief Dubs Williams is released from prison to help Max Winters bust a car theft ring, Max learns that to catch a thief, get in bed with one. (978-1-62639-239-7)

Dragon Horse War by D. Jackson Leigh. A priestess of peace and a fiery warrior must defeat a vicious uprising that entwines their destinies and ultimately their hearts. (978-1-62639-240-3)

For the Love of Cake by Erin Dutton. When everything is on the line, and one taste can break a heart, will pastry chefs

Maya and Shannon take a chance on reality? (978-1-62639-241-0)

Betting on Love by Alyssa Linn Palmer. A quiet country-girl-at-heart and a live-life-to-the-fullest biker take a risk at offering each other their hearts. (978-1-62639-242-7)

The Deadening by Yvonne Heidt. The lines between good and evil, right and wrong, have always been blurry for Shade. When Raven's actions force her to choose, which side will she come out on? (978-1-62639-243-4)

Ordinary Mayhem by Victoria A. Brownworth. Faye Blakemore has been taking photographs since she was ten, but those same photographs threaten to destroy everything she knows and everything she loves. (978-1-62639-315-8)

One Last Thing by Kim Baldwin & Xenia Alexiou. Blood is thicker than pride. The final book in the Elite Operative Series brings together foes, family, and friends to start a new order. (978-1-62639-230-4)

Songs Unfinished by Holly Stratimore. Two aspiring rock stars learn that falling in love while pursuing their dreams can be harmonious—if they can only keep their pasts from throwing them out of tune. (978-1-62639-231-1)

Beyond the Ridge by L.T. Marie. Will a contractor and a horse rancher overcome their family differences and find common ground to build a life together? (978-1-62639-232-8)

Swordfish by Andrea Bramhall. Four women battle the demons from their pasts. Will they learn to let go, or will happiness be forever beyond their grasp? (978-1-62639-233-5)

The Fiend Queen by Barbara Ann Wright. Princess Katya and her consort Starbride must turn evil against evil in order to banish Fiendish power from their kingdom, and only love will pull them back from the brink. (978-1-62639-234-2)

Up the Ante by PJ Trebelhorn. When Jordan Stryker and Ashley Noble meet again fifteen years after a short-lived affair, are either of them prepared to gamble on a chance at love? (978-1-62639-237-3)

Speakeasy by MJ Williamz. When mob leader Helen Byrne sets her sights on the girlfriend of Al Capone's right-hand man, passion and tempers flare on the streets of Chicago. (978-1-62639-238-0)

Venus in Love by Tina Michele. Morgan Blake can't afford any distractions and Ainsley Dencourt can't afford to lose control—but the beauty of life and art usually lies in the unpredictable strokes of the artist's brush. (978-1-62639-220-5)

Rules of Revenge by AJ Quinn. When a lethal operative on a collision course with her past agrees to help a CIA analyst on a critical assignment, the encounter proves explosive in ways neither woman anticipated. (978-1-62639-221-2)

The Romance Vote by Ali Vali. Chili Alexander is a sought-after campaign consultant who isn't prepared when her boss's daughter, Samantha Pellegrin, comes to work at the firm and shakes up Chili's life from the first day. (978-1-62639-222-9)

Advance: Exodus Book One by Gun Brooke. Admiral Dael Caydoc's mission to find a new homeworld for the Oconodian people is hazardous, but working with the infuriating Commander Aniwyn "Spinner" Seclan endangers her heart and soul. (978-1-62639-224-3)

UnCatholic Conduct by Stevie Mikayne. Jil Kidd goes undercover to investigate fraud at St. Marguerite's Catholic School, but life gets complicated when her student is killed—and she begins to fall for her prime target. (978-1-62639-304-2)

Season's Meetings by Amy Dunne. Catherine Birch reluctantly ventures on the festive road trip from hell with beautiful stranger Holly Daniels only to discover the road to true love has its own obstacles to maneuver. (978-1-62639-227-4)

Myth and Magic: Queer Fairy Tales edited by Radclyffe and Stacia Seaman. Myth, magic, and monsters—the stuff of childhood dreams (or nightmares) and adult fantasies. (978-1-62639-225-0)

Nine Nights on the Windy Tree by Martha Miller. Recovering drug addict, Bertha Brannon, is an attorney who is trying to stay clean when a murder sends her back to the bad end of town. (978-1-62639-179-6)

Driving Lessons by Annameekee Hesik. Dive into Abbey Brooks's sophomore year as she attempts to figure out the amazing, but sometimes complicated, life of a you-know-who girl at Gila High School. (978-1-62639-228-1)

Asher's Shot by Elizabeth Wheeler. Asher Price's candid photographs capture the truth, but when his success requires exposing an enemy, Asher discovers his only shot at happiness involves revealing secrets of his own. (978-1-62639-229-8)

Courtship by Carsen Taite. Love and justice—a lethal mix or a perfect match? (978-1-62639-210-6)

Against Doctor's Orders by Radclyffe. Corporate financier Presley Worth wants to shut down Argyle Community Hospital, but Dr. Harper Rivers will fight her every step of the way, if she can also fight their growing attraction. (978-1-62639-211-3)